Helena

HELENA

A NOVEL

by

EVELYN WAUGH

THE THOMAS MORE PRESS
Chicago, Illinois

This THOMAS MORE BOOKS TO LIVE edition is reprinted by arrangement with Sterling Lord Agency, Inc.

THE THOMAS MORE PRESS
205 West Monroe
Chicago, IL 60606

ISBN 0-88347-282-1

Contents

TO

Penelope Betjeman

Preface

IT IS reported (and I, for one, believe it) that some few years ago a lady prominent for her hostility to the Church returned from a visit to Palestine in a state of exultation. "I got the real low-down at last," she told her friends. "The whole story of the crucifixion was made up by a British woman named Ellen. Why, the guide showed me the very place where it happened. Even the priests admit it. They call their chapel 'the Invention of the Cross.'"

It has not been my primary aim to disillusion this famous lady but to retell an old story.

This is a novel.

The novelist deals with the experiences which excite his imagination. In this case the experience was my desultory reading in History and Archaeology. The resulting book, of course, is neither History nor Archaeology. Where the authorities are doubtful, I have often chosen the picturesque in preference to the plausible; I have once or twice, where they are silent, freely invented; but there is nothing, I believe, contrary to authentic history (save for certain wilful, obvious anachronisms which are introduced as a literary device), and there is little that has not some support from tradition or from early documents.

The reader may reasonably enquire: how much is true? The Age of Constantine is strangely obscure. Most of the dates and hard facts, confidently given in the encyclopaedias, soften and dissolve on examination. The life of St. Helena begins and ends in surmise and legend. We may take it as certain that she was the mother of Constantine by Constantius Chlorus; that she was proclaimed Empress by her son; that she was in Rome in 326 when Crispus, Licinianus and Fausta were murdered; that she went soon after to Jerusalem and associated herself with building the churches at Bethlehem and Olivet. It is almost certain that she directed excavations in which pieces of wood were found, which she and all Christendom immediately accepted as the cross on which Our Lord died; that she took part away, with many other relics, and left part at Jerusalem; that she lived some of her life at Nish, in Dalmatia and at Trèves. Some hagiographers have fancied her at Nicaea in 325. We do not know that.

We do not know where she was born or when. Britain is as likely a place as any other and British historians used always to claim her. We do not know that Constantius visited Britain in 273, for we have no details of his early life. His position and abilities would have qualified him to be the emissary to Tetricus, but it is pure guesswork to represent him as so employed. Helenopolis (Drepanum), on the Bosphorus, claimed to be Helena's birthplace on the grounds of its name, but Constantine was whimsical in these displays of family feeling. He named at least one other town (in Spain) after his mother, and for his sister, Constantia, he renamed the port of Maiouma in Palestine, where she cannot conceivably have been born. In preferring Colchester to York I have been guided by the picturesque. The date — as all dates in this age — is uncertain. Helena's panegyrist describes her as past eighty when she went to Jerusalem, but I have taken this as a pious exaggeration.

We do not know that the wood Helena found is the True Cross. We need make no difficulty about the possibility of its preservation, for the distance in time between Helena and Our Lord is not greater than between ourselves and King Charles I, but if we do accept its authenticity we must, I think, allow an element of the miraculous in its discovery and identification. We do know that most of the relics

of the True Cross now venerated in various places
have a clear descent from the relic venerated in the
first half of the fourth century. It used to be believed
by the vulgar that there were enough pieces of this
"true cross" to build a battleship. In the last century
a French savant, Charles Rohault de Fleury, went to
the great trouble of measuring them all. He found
a total of 4,000,000 cubic millimetres, whereas the
cross on which Our Lord suffered would probably
comprise some 178,000,000. As far as volume goes,
therefore, there is no strain on the credulity of the
faithful.

The following names are entirely fictitious: Marcias,
Calpurnia, Carpicius, Emolphus.

The Wandering Jew has no previous connexion
with Helena. I have brought them together as a
device for reconciling two discrepant stories of the
invention: one, that Helena was led to the spot in
a dream; the second and less creditable version,
that she extorted the information from an elderly
rabbi by putting him down a well and leaving him
there for a week.

In rather the same way I have given Constantius
Chlorus a mistress, although he was reputed to be
unusually chaste. One historian makes Helena an
elderly concubine from Drepanum. I contrived the

drowned Bithynian as a hint to the knowing that I thought nothing of the credibility of this tale.

There are some other echoes and reflexions of this kind scattered about the following pages, but it would be tedious to point them out. They are there to be found by anyone whom they amuse.

The story is just something to be read; in fact a legend.

Helena

CHAPTER ONE

Court Memoir

ONCE, very long ago, before ever the flowers were named which struggled and fluttered below the rain-swept walls, there sat at an upper window a princess and a slave reading a story which even then was old: or, rather, to be entirely prosaic, on the wet afternoon of the Nones of May in the year (as it was computed later) of Our Lord 273, in the city of Colchester, Helena, red-haired, youngest daughter of Coel, Paramount Chief of the Trinovantes, gazed into the rain while her tutor read the *Iliad* of Homer in a Latin paraphrase.

Recessed there in the fortification they might have seemed an incongruous couple. The princess was taller and lighter than the general taste required; her hair, sometimes golden in the sunlight, was more often dull copper in her cloudy home; her eyes had a boyish melancholy; the mood—at once resentful, abstracted, and yet very remotely tinged with awe —of British youth in contact with the Classics. There would be decades in the coming seventeen centuries, when she would have been thought beautiful; born too soon, she was, here in Colchester, among her own people, dubbed the plain one.

Her tutor certainly regarded her with aversion as, at once, the symbol of his low condition and the daily task which made that condition irksome. He went by the name of Marcias and was then in the prime of what seemed his manhood; swarthy skin, black beard, beak-nose and home-sick eyes spoke of his exotic origin; winter and summer his rheumy cough protested against his exile. Hunting days were his solace when the princess was away from dawn to sunset and he, left sole lord of the schoolroom, could write his letters. These letters were his life; elegant, esoteric, speculative, rhapsodic, they travelled the world from Spain to Bithynia, from free rhetorician to servile poet. They got talked about and had brought Coel more than one offer for his purchase. He was one of the younger intellectuals, but here fate had landed him, in drizzle and draught, the property of a convivial, minor royalty, the daily companion of an adolescent girl. There was no taint of impropriety in their conjunction, for in his boyhood a precocious and transitory taste for the ballet had once caused Marcias to be assigned for the

Eastern market and he had been suitably pruned by the surgeon.

"*And Helen of the white arms, fair among women, let fall a round tear and veiled her face in shining linen; and Aithre, daughter of Pitheus and the ox-eyed Klymene, attended her to the Scaean Gate.* Do you think I read this to amuse myself?"

"It is only the fishermen," said Helena, "coming up from the sea for tonight's beano. There's basketfuls of oysters. Sorry; go on about the ox-eyed Klymene."

"*And Priam, sitting among the elders of his court said: 'Small wonder that Trojans and Greeks are in arms for Princess Helen. She breathes the air of high Olympus. Sit, dear child; this war is not thine, but of the Immortals.'*"

"Priam was a sort of relation of ours, you know."

"So I have heard your father frequently observe."

From this sheltered room on a clear day one could descry the sea, but now the distance was lost in mist which, even as she watched, closed swiftly over marsh and pasture, villas and huts, over the baths where the District Commander and his new guest had lately entered, till it filled the ditch and lapped the walls below her; on such a day Helena thought, not for the first time—for such days were common in her bright Springtide—on such a day the hill-town, which rose so modestly above the fens, might stand in the clouds among the high winds of the mountains and these squat battlements might over-hang a limitless gulf; and while with half her mind she heard the voice behind her—*"For she did not know that these, her twin brethren, lay fast in Sparta, in their own land, under the life-giving earth"*—she half-sought an eagle mounting from the white void below.

Then the swift squall passed and the fog reopened, bringing her back, within a few feet to earth. Only the brick cupola of the baths remained obscure, bound in its own exhalation of steam and smoke. How near the ground they sat!

"Were the Trojan walls taller than ours at Col-chester?"

"Oh, yes; I think so."

"Much?"

"Very much."

"Have you seen them?"

"They were destroyed utterly in the olden days."

"Nothing left, Marcias? Nothing to mark where they stood?"

"There's a modern town the tourists flock to. The guides will show you anything you ask for—the tomb of Achilles, Paris's carved bed, the wooden leg of the great horse. But of Troy itself there is nothing left but poetry."

"I don't see," said Helena, looking out along the sturdy face of the masonry, "how they could ever quite destroy a city."

"The world is very old, Helena, and full of ruins. Here in a young country like Britain you may find that hard to realize, but in the East there are heaps of sand which were once great cities. They are thought to be unlucky. Even the wandering tribes keep clear of them for fear of ghosts."

"I shouldn't be afraid," said Helena. "Why don't people dig? Some of Troy's bound to be there still, hidden underneath the tourists' town. When I am educated I shall go and find the real Troy—Helen's."

"Plenty of ghosts there, Helena. The poets have never let those heroes sleep in peace."

The slave turned back to the manuscript but before he could resume reading, Helena asked: "Do you think, Marcias, they could ever destroy Rome?"

"Why not?"

"Well, I hope they don't; not yet, anyway. Not before I've had the chance to go and look round— Do you know, I have never in my life met anyone who's actually been to The City?"

"Few cross from Gaul to Italy now, since the troubles."

"I'm going one day. The barbarian prisoners, you know, in the colossal theatre fight with elephants. Have you ever seen an elephant, Marcias?"

"No."

"They're as big as six horses."

"So I believe."

"I'm going to see everything for myself one day, when I'm educated."

"My child, no one knows where he is going. I hoped once to go to Alexandria. I have a friend there whom I have never seen, a most sophistical man. We have so much to say to one another that cannot be written. The Museum was to have bought me. Instead they sent me North and sold me in Cologne to the Immortal Tetricus and he sent me here as a present to your father."

"Perhaps, when I am educated, papa will set you free."

"He talks of it sometimes, after dinner. But what is freedom, to be given and taken? Freedom to be a soldier and to be ordered here and there and cut down in the end by the barbarians in a bog or a forest; freedom to amass a fortune so great that the Immortal Emperor covets it and sends his executioner to collect it? I have my own secret freedom, Helena. What more can your father give me?"

"Well, a trip to Alexandria to see your sophistical chum."

"The mind of man has no legal status. Who can say which is the more free, I or the Immortal Emperor?"

"I sometimes think, you know," said Helena, leaving her tutor sailing free and wide in the void which he made his chilly home, "that it was a good deal more agreeable being an Immortal in Helen's time than it is now. Do you know what has happened to the Immortal Valerian? Papa told me last evening as a great joke. They have him on show in Persia, *stuffed*."

"Perhaps," said the slave, "we are all immortal."

"Perhaps," said the princess, "we are all slaves."

"Sometimes, my child, you make startlingly intelligent observations."

"Marcias, have you seen the new staff-officer who arrived from Gaul? It is for him that papa is giving the banquet tonight."

"All of us slaves—to the earth, 'the life-giving earth.' They are talking now about a Way and a

Word; a Way of purification, a Word of enlightenment. It is all the rage in Antioch, I hear, where they have more than twenty genuine Indian sages at work teaching a new way of breathing."

"He is very pale and serious. I'm sure he's employed in some very secret and important mission."

Meanwhile in the hot-room the District Commander was occupied, less complacently, with the same thought. All over, except where numerous scars recorded his service on the frontier, the General was red and healthily sweating; it was a tough old body, much chopped about, lacking a finger here, a toe there, the free use of a tendon somewhere else, but the face under his bald and dewy head retained the puzzled innocence of early youth. Opposite him, in the torrid twilight, like a corpse in a mortuary, lay Constantius, as pale as when he entered, damp and white and wiry, still asking questions. He had asked questions ever since he had arrived two days ago, respectfully as befitted a junior officer, insistently as one who had a right to know; pertinent, delicate questions on topics which, if raised at all between a senior or a junior officer, should have been raised by the General.

"Shocking business about the Divine Valerian," said the District Commander, seeking to turn the conversation to wider interests.

"Very shocking, sir."

"First a mounting-block, then a footstool, now a dummy, skinned, tanned, stuffed full of straw, swinging from the rafters for the Persians to poke fun at. I only heard the full story the other day."

"Yes, it's had the most disastrous effect on our prestige in the East," said Constantius. "I was in Persia last winter and found things very sticky. Do you think, if the news gets about, it's likely to have any effect on the frontier legions—the Second Augusta, for instance? How is the morale of the Second Augusta?"

"Splendid body of men. Only wish they could have a cut at the Persians; they'd show them."

"Are they? Do you? That's very interesting. We had rather disquieting reports of the Second Augusta. Wasn't there some trouble in November about their winter quarters?"

"No," said the General.

"Well, we can safely leave the Persians to the Immortal Aurelian." Constantius rose from his slab of marble. "I'll see you in the tepid-room, sir."

The General grunted and turned on his face, glad to be rid of the fellow yet resentful of his manner of going; when he had joined under the Divine Gordian, junior officers had deferred to their seniors or known the reason why.

"Depend upon it," thought the General, unhappy at this, by long habit, the happiest hour of the day, when the annoyances of the flesh welled up and were washed away, when the stiff old muscles relaxed and deep inside him he felt the digestive juices flowing fresh and expectant of dinner; "depend upon it that fellow is up to something."

Constantius's papers were in order, under Tetricus's own seal; a liaison officer on a routine tour of the province. "Routine my eye," thought the General. Who was this "we" who knew so much and wanted to know so much more? "Not Tetricus, or I'm a Pict," thought the General. How had "we" come to hear of that disgraceful business of the Second Augusta at Chester? The General clapped his hands and the slave brought, ready prepared for him, the draught he always took at about this hour; cold, Celtic beer spiced with ginger and cinnamon, a beverage the General had taught them to make; it had the property of simultaneously creating and satisfying thirst; the General drank deeply and rubbed his old flanks.

When at length he marched to the tepid-room Constantius had finished his massage.

"I'll see you in the cool-room, sir," he said and took the cold plunge, not, as the General did, with many frank hissings and splutterings, but calmly and deliberately descending the steps one by one as though to some religious lustration, and emerging into the hot towels, swathing himself in them, and proceeding sedately to his couch in the hall beyond as though vested for the altar.

The slaves knew every inch of the General's body but they seldom got through the afternoon's rubbing without a fair amount of cursing. Today the General was fretful but silent. He wallowed briefly in the cold water then, his mind resolved, sought the couch next to Constantius. A question greeted him before he was fully settled.

"This fellow Coel we're dining with this evening; what sort of fellow is he, sir?"

"You'll see for yourself. He's all right. Perhaps he lacks Gravity."

"Is he of any importance in local politics?"

"Politics," said the General, "politics"; and then after a pause he said what he had made up his mind to say when he lay alone in the hot-room. "You'll find Britain in a highly prosperous state, more so, I daresay, than any province in the Empire, and the reason is that we don't go in for politics over here. We come under Gaul and we take our orders from there, provided they don't give us too many; when they do, we just seem to forget about them. Posthumus, Lollianus, Victorinus, Victoria, Marius, Tetricus—they're all one to us."

"Would you say, sir, that Tetricus has a considerable following among—?"

"Just a minute, young man, I haven't finished what I was saying.

"I've been a regimental soldier all my life until they retired me here. I've never gone in for politics or for intelligence or for special missions. You've asked me a lot of questions in the last two days and I haven't asked you one. I haven't asked you who you are or what you want. Your letters say you are a member of Tetricus's staff; that's quite good enough for me. As I've told you, I've never gone in for secret service work and it's too late now, but I'm not quite a fool yet. Allow me to give a little advice. Next time you want to pass yourself off as a member of Tetricus's staff, don't boast about making trips to Persia, and if you want me to think you come from Cologne don't pick your personal guard from a legion that has served on the Danube for the last fifteen years.

"And now, if you will excuse an old man's infirmity, I propose to sleep."

"And Aphrodite caught up Paris in a cloud of darkness and bore him to his own fragrant and high-vaulted chamber and herself sought Helen where she stood among her women above the Scaean Gate. She plucked her perfumed gown and said: 'Come, Paris is waiting on his carved bed, radiant, delicately clad as though he were resting from the dance'. And Helen, daughter of Zeus, slipped away from her attendant women and stood in her shining veil in Paris's room. Laughter-loving Venus set a chair for her by the bed, and Helen said: 'Would you had fallen in battle.' But Paris answered: 'We too have Immortal allies. Come. My love is sweet and hot as the day I took ship with you from Sparta, as the night on sea-girt Kranae where I first knew you. Come.' So they lay together on the fretted bed while beyond the walls Menelaus roamed like a wild beast seeking for Paris and finding him not in all the watching host. Neither Greek nor Trojan would hide Paris for they hated him as they hated black Death itself and while he lay heedless, King Agamemnon proclaimed Menelaus the victor and fair Helen forfeit."

"What a lark!" said Princess Helena. "What a sell! Can't you just see Menelaus ramping and raging about and being smacked on the back by everyone and Agamemnon pompously declaring him the winner? And there was Helen tucked up with Paris all the time. Oh, what sucks!"

"It is an incident quite inconsistent with the heroic virtues," said Marcias. "For that reason the great Longinus considers it the interpolation of a later hand."

"Ah," said Helena, "the *Great Longinus*."

He was a figure half of fun to her, this stupendous pundit, half of awe; her second heroic myth. The first was her nurse's father, a sapper-sergeant slain by the Picts; she never tired, as a child, of stories of his valour and integrity and when she was translated from nursery to schoolroom, Longinus inappropriately took a place beside him; Marcias paid him more than filial homage; his name occurred hourly, at every lesson. Omniscient, polymath, throned in the remote splendours of Palmyra, Longinus had become invested in her mind with the legends of her race, identified with those white-robed men of the sickle and the mistletoe whose garbled lore was still whispered in the kitchen quarters. These dissimilar paragons were the twin deities of her adolescence; she had a homely, humorous intimacy with them, but also awe.

The snores of the District Commander still rang through the dome while Constantius neatly dressed himself and went alone through the rain and mire to the city gates.

"There he goes," said Helena, "the man of mystery, the beauty."

When he reached his quarters he called the commander of his guard.

"Corporal-major, the men are to take down their regimental numerals immediately."

"Very good, sir."

"And, corporal-major, impress on them the need for absolute security. If anyone asks any questions, they're from the Rhine."

"They've been told, sir."

"Well, tell them again. If I hear anyone's been talking, I'll confine the lot to barracks."

Then Constantius called his valet and his hairdresser and set about such adornments for dinner as were possible to a field-officer travelling light, on confidential business.

The ladies did not dine with the gentlemen but

they dined extremely well; their cosier parlour lay between hall and kitchen and Helena's aunt, who ruled the household, made her own choice of the dishes before they left the charcoal and conducted them under her own eyes, succulent and piping hot, less elaborately garnished than those which appeared before the King, but with all their pure flavours unimpaired. Moreover, instead of lolling in manly style among the cushions and being fed by slaves, the ladies of the household squatted square to their victuals at a low table, rolled back their sleeves and got their hands well into the pot. The plain but abundant fare comprised oysters stewed with saffron, boiled crabs, soles fried in butter, sucking-pig seethed in milk, roast capons, titbits of lamb spitted between slices of onion, a simple, sweet confection of honey and eggs and cream, and a deep Samian pitcher of home-brewed mead; it would not have done in Italy or Egypt but it was well-suited to the British ladies' taste and circumstances.

"What a spread!" said Princess Helena, when she had guzzled. "What a blow-out!"

The ladies were putting themselves in order for the concert. Helena's hair which at her lesson had hung in thick russet plaits was now maturely dressed and bedizened; she wore a robe of embroidered silk which had come to her by dromedary and ship and pack mule and porter from distant China; her narrow slippers shone with stones and gold thread and when she had washed her hands and white fore-arms—*"Helen of the white arms, fair among women,"* she thought as she dabbled in the steaming lime-water—she planted all sixteen various rings that had been the youngest sister's share of her mother's jewel-chest, firmly on her strong young fingers.

"You look perfectly charming, child," said her aunt, adjusting the fillet on Helena's brow. "We won't go in quite yet. The gentlemen have just gone to be sick."

Presently the ladies of the royal house made their entry. *"Helen, fair among women, daughter of aegis-bearing Zeus,"* thought Helena, as, last but tallest of the line, behind her aunt, her father's three mistresses, her three married and two unmarried sisters, Helena saluted her father. He waved to them generally and genially from his couch and they took their places at the side of the room on their ten stiff chairs.

Then the orchestra struck up, three strings and a wayward pipe, and the singers—first one, then another, at haphazard it seemed; finally all eight of the patriarchal basses—joined their full lungs in the opening dirge.

"I expect you are used to this kind of thing," said the District Commander privately to Constantius.

"To nothing quite like this."

"We have it whenever Coel gives a party. It lasts for hours."

The first direful sounds raised the King, who had already shown abundant pleasure in his entertainment, to evident transports. "My favourite piece," he explained; "the lament for my ancestors. We usually start with it. Like all true art it has the merit of prodigious length. Of course since it is in our native tongue, some of it may be lost on you. I will tell you when anything particularly fine is said. At the moment they are treating of the foundation of my family in remote, almost legendary, times by the irregular alliance of the river Scamander with the nymph Idaea. Listen."

High and thin and heartless sang the fiddles and the chanter; deep and turgid and lachrimose sang the bearded choristers. Lax and supine sprawled the soldiers; rigid and erect sat the royal women. Softly the page stepped from couch to couch with the mead-bowl; heavily the District Commander stumbled once more to the vomitorium.

Uncouth, hypnotic, the voices filled the hall from coffered roof to mosaic pavement and carried far into the night their tale of death.

"Brutus, great-grandson of Aeneas, has now reached Britain," said Coel at length; "we have almost, you might say, reached modern times. He is the real father of our race. He found the whole island quite empty, you know, except for a few old giants. After Brutus the story becomes much more circumstantial."

None of King Coel's family, it appeared, had died naturally; few even plausibly. One took doctored wine at the hands of his step-daughter and ran horribly amok in the forest, naked, tearing up young trees and frightening the wolves and bears. And his was by no means the most alarming case. All the bereavements of that ancient and tuneless family—classic myth, Celtic fairy tale and stark history—mingled and swelled inharmoniously, among the cooking smells and lamp smells and the heavy smell of mead.

Constantius was a man of temperate habits; he had seen more than one officer gormandize himself out of fine prospects in the days of the Divine Gallienus; but he had drunk deep that night, so that

the sharp pain of the entertainment was dulled and
he lay bemused, borne out of himself by the fumes
of liquor, so that he looked down on all his talents,
neatly displayed like cut gems on the engraver's
tray, and saw himself almost as he was. There was
little self-love in Constantius; others, not he, in
the last two centuries had been consumed by that
master-passion; others, now the peers and playmates
of the gods, had died of that sickness. Constantius
in his own eyes fell short of perfection. His talents
comprised all that was needed—no more; a repre-
sentative collection, not unique, but adequate; he
would make do. His need was simple; not today, not
tomorrow, but soon, sometime before he grew too
old to make proper use of it, Constantius wanted the
World.

"They are singing of the flagellation of Boadicea,"
said Coel; "rather a delicate subject to us Romans,
but very dear to my simple people."

The recital was scarcely less familiar to Helena
than to her father; she withdrew from the catalogue
of mortality and, eupeptically, indulged a fantasy
she had cherished since childhood. Perhaps each
of the women had some such secret, interior pastime,
so still they sat on their ten severe thrones. Helena
was playing horses, a game which began with her

first pony; a breathless, wordless steeple-chase across impassable superequine obstacles, splendidly leapt, and endless stretches of resilient sward. Helena had galloped thus in solitude hours without number, but of late years, as her womanhood broke bud, a keener excitement infused the game. Two played it now. There was the will of the rider that spoke down the length of the rein, from the gloved hand to the warm and tender tongue under the bit; articulate, coaxing, commanding, now barely sensible, light as an eyelid, now steel-hard and compelling; that spoke in the stab of the spur and sudden double smart of the whip. And there was the will of the animal to shrink and start, to toss aside the restraint of bridle and saddle and the firm legs across her, to shake the confident equipoise, awake him to the intense life and the will to combat under him; leaving him nothing of what he took for granted, draw more from him until he put the whole of himself into the tussle. Then at the height of the play, in sweat and blood-flecked foam, came the sweet moment of surrender, the fusion, and the two were off together, single, full-stretch over the resounding earth, as they had raced in childhood, with none but the wind to oppose them. She took some handling, the chestnut.

Thus Helena galloped while through the hypo-caustic air the death-song of her ancestors rumbled and wailed.

"They are singing of Cymbeline," said the King.

Presently the hand on the rein steadied her, pressed her gently back into a walk, then patted her neck and she shook in answer the silver ornaments of her harness. They strolled together, hand-in-hand, as it were, like a courting couple along the water-side, until a slight shift of weight, a pressure from the leg, a gathering up of attention in the thrilling touch on the lip, set her once more stepping briskly out in the glades of her keen, young mind.

The dirge ended and the singers' throats now gurgled with mead; the piper shook out the spittle and the fiddlers tinkered with their strings. The King's applause momentarily awoke the company from their several reveries. Momentarily only; there was an interval of pledging and quaffing; then the music began again.

"This is a very modern song," said Coel; "it was written by the chief bard in my grandfather's day to commemorate the annihilation of the IX Legion"; and, deep in the toga, which contrary to metropolitan fashion he always wore at table, the old King rumbled with amusement.

Trotting through the limpid upper-air of her

thoughts, stepping high and delicately, nibbling the bit, tossing the buckles and sparkling bosses of her bridle, making the reins ring like a harp-string with the note of assent and exultation, tenderly, sweetly displaying before the world the chivalry of her rider; thus went Helena.

And Constantius also rode; rode in triumph; not in his chariot amid the sweat and garlic-reek of The City, not behind yoked sovereigns and exotic animals, the almoners and augurs and tumblers and ceremonial troops, not in the pantomime of official triumph; but at the head of battle-worn, victorious legions, at the heart of power, at the entry into possession; he rode between crowds who were part sullen, part timorous, part flushed with gratitude for their immediate salvation, all scanning him as he passed for a sign of what was coming to them. That was Constantius's triumph as he jogged along in his service uniform into a conquered and anxious world.

And, as he lay, he looked across the hall to the row of women; scarcely observing them, his eyes passed from one rapt face to another, until in the lowest place but highest by a handsbreadth, Helena raised hers to meet them. They gazed at one another, unknowingly, separate, then running together like drops of condensed steam on the ewer, pausing, bulging one against the other, until, suddenly, they were one and ran down in a single minute cascade. Helena trotted on and Constantius bestrode her in triumph.

Constantius had done something unprecedented and unpremeditated, something for which his talents were ill suited; he had fallen in love.

CHAPTER TWO

Fair Helen Forfeit

ON the morning after the banquet Constantius woke early and ill—it was thus that his liquor always took him even in the vinelands—and like the well-trained officer he was, he sought as soon as might be, to shift the burden of malaise on his subordinates. For weeks now he had left early stables to his corporal-major; grey, queasy mornings such as this were ordained for discipline.

As he expected, everything was behind-hand; he saw it in the corporal-major's eye as he saluted; he saw it in the men as they stood to attention; he saw it in the half-groomed horses and the disordered straw. What was more, there was a girl in the stables. He could see her back through the door of the harness-room, a red-headed girl wearing, surprisingly, a bridle. She turned towards him and removing the bit from her mouth, smiled.

"You *are* late," said Helena. "I hope you didn't mind my having a look at your bridle; the old boy in charge thought you might, but I said it would be all right. He doesn't know the first thing about horses, you know. He thinks these are Gallic."

"That's right, miss," said the corporal-major, glad at last to be on safe ground. "We're all from Gaul, troop and horses. It's in orders."

"Bet you they aren't. I'd know them anywhere. They come from Allectus's stud in the South. He sent me one once; they're quite special, you know. Aren't they?" she asked Constantius.

"You're quite right," he said, "we remounted at Silchester. What are you doing here?"

"Oh, I always go round and look at any new horses that come in."

"And try on the harness?"

"If I feel like it. I say, you do look ill."

"All right, corporal-major, carry on."

"Quite green."

"We met last night, in a way."

"Yes."

"What do you do besides hang about the stables?"

"Oh, I'm still being educated. I'm the King's daughter you know and we Britons think a lot of education. What's your name?"

"Constantius. What's yours?"

"Helena. Green-faced Constantius."

"Helen the ostler."

And so these two names, "Chlorus" and "Stabularia," lightly blown, drifted away into the dawn and settled at last among the pages of history.

Constantius had allowed no time for courtship in his itinerary. The whole British visit was supererogatory, something subsidiary to his main mission; something which, if it ever came out, would want explaining. It had seemed easy, with his other business speedily concluded and a month in hand, to slip across the Channel, to see for himself this little frequented dependency, to form his own opinions, to add to the knowledge he was patiently building up of the vast structure of imperial government, to add one or two more names to the men of consequence with whom he was on personal terms. But he had not reckoned on falling in love.

However the thing had happened and must be settled expeditiously. He presented his suit to Coel.

"It's all very well," said the King crossly, "but I don't know anything about you."

He had tried Constantius drunk and sober and he did not like him; he found him both dull and sly; dull when drunk and sly when sober. He was not at all Coel's idea of a gentleman, and the District Commander whom he had consulted as soon as this question of Helena's marriage arose, had said exactly what Coel was saying now. "I don't know anything about the fellow."

Constantius answered: "There's very little to know . . . as yet."

"Your family?"

"On that score you may rest completely satisfied."

"Yes?"

"I have reasons for remaining inconspicuous."

"Yes?"

"I can assure you that you need have no fear that the alliance I suggest is, in that respect, at all unworthy."

Coel waited for further information but none was forthcoming. At length he said: "I daresay we seem old-fashioned in Britain, but we still care a great deal for such things."

"Yes?"

Constantius turned in his mind the question that had been vexing him for some days, which he thought was decided. He had meant to keep his secret until he was clear of Britain, until he was across the Rhine, but the King was plainly not to be put off; according to Coel's simple tradition if a man had a genealogy to be proud of, he hired an orchestra and set the thing to music.

At last Constantius spoke. "You have a right to the information you seek, but I must beg you to respect my confidence. When I tell you, you will understand my hesitation. I would have preferred you to accept my word, but since you insist—" he paused to give full weight to his declaration—"I am of the Imperial Family."

It fell flat. "You are, are you?" said Coel. "It's the first I've ever heard of there being such a thing."

"I am the great-nephew of the Divine Claudius . . . Also," he added, "of the Divine Quintilius, whose reign, though brief, was entirely constitutional."

"Yes," said Coel, "and apart from their divinity, who were they? Some of the emperors we've had lately, you know, have been"—very literally—"nothing to make a song about. It's one thing burning incense to them and quite another having them in the family. You must see that."

"On my father's side," said Constantius, "I am of the old Danubian nobility."

"Yes," said Coel without interest, "all Danubians are, who I've ever met. Where's your place?"

"The family estates are enormous but they are in the hands of another branch. I myself have no property to speak of."

"No." Coel nodded and fell silent.

"I am a soldier. I live where I am sent."

"Yes," said Coel; another pause, then: "Well, I will speak to the girl. We don't arrange marriages over here quite as you do, I daresay, on the Danube. Helena shall decide."

And when Constantius heard this he smiled thinly but confidently, and so took leave of the King.

"Mead," roared Coel, "and music. No, not you" —as all the bards came bundling in—"only the three strings and the pipe. I have to think."

Presently, in a softened mood, he sent for Helena.

"I am sorry to interrupt your lessons."

"It was 'break,' papa. I had just gone to the stables to look at Pylades's over-reach. He'll be all right for Tuesday."

"Helena, I have had a most impudent request from that sickly-looking young staff-officer. He wants to marry you."

"Yes, papa."

"A relation of the Divine What-d'you-call-him— awful fellow who was Emperor not long ago. Says he comes from the Balkans somewhere. You don't really want to marry him, do you?"

"Yes, papa."

"Stop. Go away," said Coel suddenly to his

band. "Take the bowl; be off," he said to the slave. The music died among the rafters; slippers shuffled among the rushes and the room was silent. "Stop fiddling with that thing," he said to Helena.

"It is only a curb chain. The hook's got bent."

"Put it away. Not there"—as Helena tucked it down the front of her tunic.

"Gone now," she said, wriggled her shoulders to dispose the steel more comfortably between her breasts, and stood erect; only her fingers behind her back twiddled. "I have to marry someone, sometime, you know," she said.

"I can't for the life of me think why. I have never regarded you as a girl."

"Oh, papa."

"It's different with your sisters, fine, plump girls, who know all about cooking and sewing. I get offers for them every week. But you, Helena; well I never expected this. You look like a boy, you ride like a boy. Your tutor tells me you have a masculine mind, whatever he means by that. I did think you at least might stay at home with your old father. And if you must marry, why choose a foreigner? Oh yes, I know we're all Roman citizens and all that; so are a lot of Jews and Egyptians and disgusting Germans. They're just foreigners to me. You won't like living abroad, you know."

"I must go with Constantius, papa, wherever he goes. Besides, he's promised to take me to The City."

"The City indeed! Ask the District Commander. He met a fellow who'd been there. Told him all about it. *Awful* place."

"I must see for myself, papa."

"You'll never get there. No one goes there nowadays who can possibly help it—even the Divine Emperors. You'll be stuck all your life in some Balkan barracks, you see."

"I must go with Constantius. After all, papa, we Trojans are always in exile, aren't we—poor banished children of Teucer?"

Then King Coel suffered a change of mind which in a less sanguine man might be called despair, and turned his attention to the wedding celebrations.

Constantius was eager to be off, overseas, to his work; there was no time for the sewing-maids to prepare the robes of a King's daughter, no time for the heralds to assemble the kin; time only for the augurs to fix a lucky day, a day of high, salt wind and momentary sunshine. The ox was duly felled

and the Spring-flowers of his garland lay with him
in the temple court-yard, crushed and bloody on the
sanded floor; in the porch bride and groom broke
the wheaten cake and, as they entered the sanctuary
to burn incense to the gods and the Divine Aurelian,
the royal bards sang the epithalamium which had
been taught and learned, father to son, before the
gods of Rome were known in the island.

In the hall bride and bridegroom sat enthroned
until sunset while the court and the garrison feasted
round them. In twilight they were led to Constantius's lodging; he took her in his arms and carried
her across the threshold of the home that was neither
his nor hers; a soldier's camping-place. His baggage
was already in order for the journey and stood
stacked by the bed.

The music and voices of the banquet came clearly
to them through the mist.

"I have given the guard leave till reveille," said
Constantius. "I hope they make the best of it.
They've some hard travelling ahead."

Presently the revellers came out with torches and
sang round the house. Helena picked her way to the
window, barefoot through the baggage. Standing
there, she could see only the golden globes of flame
moving below in the mist.

"The minstrels, Chlorus. Come and look."

But Constantius lay still, invisible in the lampless room behind her.

The song came to its end; Helena watched the torches dwindle in the darkness, glimmer and expire, heard the voices die to a murmur and fall at last quite silent. The marriage-house seemed to stand solitary in the night and fog.

"It is like being alone on an island, isn't it? Like 'sea-girt Kranae.' "

"Kranae?" said Chlorus. "Kranae? I don't think I know the place. Is it one of the islands of Britain?"

And Helena turned back to her husband.

Next day, while Constantius despatched the advanced-party and distributed the pack-loads, Helena went hunting once more for the last time over the familiar country. The timber round Colchester had been cut, first for reasons of defence, later for fuel; coverts of scrub and second-growth extended from below the walls, growing sparse and bare in successive belts as they approached the forests; the roads too had been cleared against ambush; there were large estates of tilled land and stretches of marsh towards the sea which gave free passage to the nimble game but engulfed horse and rider; there the hounds had to be whipped off the scent. It was a difficult country requiring cleverness and long experience in huntsmen and hounds; sometimes the game fell to the spears at the covert-side; sometimes the hounds got away and pulled him down in the forest; the huntsman's skill lay in driving him up the lanes into the open inland.

It was a day of promise, the mist rose early leaving a wet and windless country and a strong scent. "Just the day we've been asking for, miss—I should say, madam," said the head huntsman. Helena rode Pylades; she sat astride and the saddle-tree solaced her man-made hurt; whip in hand, rein in hand, the air of her home sweet in her nostrils. The smell of the hunt, compact of horse-sweat and warm harness, new leaf and old leaf trodden together; the call of the horn; the horse-life under her, between her thighs, at her fingers' ends; everything of that tangy British morning contended with the memories of the night and seemed in those last few free hours to heal her maidenhead.

It was a mixed bag—two grey old boars that bolted, wheeled, charged and fell to the javelin throwers, a fallow hind whom the hounds followed slowly, with many checks, who at last led them a clear run to her death in the bare cornlands and, after noon, a red deer, rare in those parts, a beast in his splendid prime, four-atop and all his rights, who ran to the sea in a great half-circle and fell to the hounds on the shingle at the water's edge.

Only Helena was with the huntsmen at the kill. The Roman followers were lost and forgotten. The little cavalcade turned towards home into the setting sun; two of the hounds were lame but Pylades trotted bravely towards his stable; as she jogged back through the dear, darkling country the exhilaration of the morning was all spent. It was night when they reached the town.

That evening Helena said to her father: "I suppose my education is finished now?"

"Yes," said Coel, "finished."

"What's going to happen to Marcias?"

A remote and rather kindly look came over the King's face. "Marcias?" he said. "Marcias. I've always been very fond of Marcias. Clever fellow. Wasted as a girl's tutor."

"You used sometimes to say, papa, that you'd free him when my education was finished."

"Did I? Did I say that? I don't think I ever said anything quite as definite as that. Besides, how was I to know your education would be over so soon? There's plenty of good work in Marcias yet."

"I think he wants to go to Alexandria, papa."

"I'm sure he does. And think how bad it would be for him. I've heard all about Alexandria—beastly place; nothing but sophists and aesthetes. I like Marcias. We have obligations towards him. I'd keep him myself but he's not exactly in my line."

"Will you give him to me, papa?"

"My dear child, he'd be completely out of place in a garrison town. He'll fetch a good price in Gaul; you see if he doesn't."

CHAPTER THREE

None but My Foe to Be My Guide

CONSTANTIUS CHLORUS was a bad sailor; he lay below muffled in his military cloak while Helena night-long strode the deck, saw the stars swing into view above the dipping sails, blaze and darken and appear anew; saw at length the whole sky lighten, the line of fire arch and rise until the whole sun stood clear over the water and it was full day; watched the sailors busy with the sheets, got into talk with them, lent them a hand, squatted with them round the forecastle brazier and shared their broiled fish. "Was it thus," she wondered, rinsing her scaly fingers in a bucket of sea-water and drying them in her lap, "was it thus, perhaps, that Paris brought his stolen queen to Ilium?"

Land came to sight at noon; soon she could descry the glittering citadel of the foreign port and the haze of wood-smoke along the water-front; soon they were abreast of the beacon and the ship, suddenly quiet in all her creaking rigging, slipped into the still water of the harbour; a single authoritative voice from the mole directed them to their mooring; they struck sail, dropped anchor and a host of bum-boats clustered alongside; their masts made part of a grove of shipping silently riding at anchor in the afternoon sun.

Constantius Chlorus came on deck and looked knowingly at the sun. "Boulogne at last. We've made a good passage. Those must be part of Carausius's fleet; the fastest ships in the Channel. Not a pirate can touch them. I must look Carausius up this evening if he's in the town."

"We've been talking about him; Ben says he could take over the whole of Britain any time he wanted to."

"And who, pray, is the astute Ben?"

"Ben's the bosun. He says whoever rules the Channel, rules Britain. He's got three sons, all at sea."

"Helena, I don't want you to start picking up stray friends and gossiping."

"Why not? I always do."

"Well, for one thing, I don't want people to know where I've been or where you've come from."

"Everyone knows where I come from."

"No, Helena, not here; still less across the Rhine. I've been meaning to tell you. As soon as we cross the Rhine into Swabia, there must be no talk of Gaul or Britain. No one must know about this journey of mine. Do you understand?''

''But aren't we going to Rome?''

''Not yet.''

''But you said . . .''

''Not yet. A time will come. You shall go to Rome, but not yet.''

''But where are we going now?''

''You are going to Nish.''

The word fell between them, inert, ponderous, amorphous.

''Nish?''

''Surely you've heard of Nish?''

''No, Constantius, never.''

''It is where Uncle Claudius fought his great battle with the Goths.''

''Yes.''

''One of the most glorious victories—not five years ago.''

'You say *I* am going to this place. Are you not coming?''

''Soon. I have business first elsewhere. You'll be better at Nish.''

''Is it far?''

''A month or six weeks. The couriers used to do it in a fortnight. That was in the old days when the post-stages were properly organized with the best horses in the Empire waiting fresh every twenty miles and the roads safe to ride at night. Things aren't so good now; we'll get all that tidied up soon. But you'll do it in a month. Or you might wait at Ratisbon and come on with me later. I shall know better in a day or two."

"And is—is Nish far from Rome?"

"It's on the way to Rome," said Constantius. "Not directly, perhaps. One does not travel direct to Rome."

"They say all roads lead there."

"Mine does, by way of Nish."

The corporal-major reported for orders; Constantius left Helena's side and she wandered forward and leaning on the bulwark studied the view, so like that which she had seen yesterday as she looked her last on her native shore, the taverns and warehouses of the water-front, the smoky huddle of huts behind them, the ashlar walls of the citadel and the columned temple crowning all; so foreign, the gate to a new life, the starting-point of the road so smoothly metalled, so straight, so devious, that led to Nish, to Rome, and whither beyond?

They travelled fast, saddling before dawn, bivouacking for their midday meal at the roadside, sleeping where darkness found them at the nearest stage-post. Constantius eschewed the towns. On the evening they reached Châlons they spent the night at a rough little inn outside the walls and cantered over the bridge at daybreak before the town was awake. At the border-castle of Strasbourg Constantius had friends with the VIII Legion; they stayed in the commander's quarters but Helena was sent early to bed and Constantius sat up all night talking soberly; next morning his face was paler than ever and grim with fatigue; he scarcely spoke until they were across the Rhine; then, suddenly, his hard mood relaxed. The change touched the men and through them the horses and they jogged along in the sunshine at ease, almost merrily. The troopers sang snatches of bawdy ditties; they halted early, unsaddled, turned the horses to grass at hobble, and lay full length while the smoke of their fire rose straight into the windless sky.

"I'm coming with you as far as Ratisbon," said Constantius. "I have the time. Then I must go back to Châlons. I have business there."

"Will it take long?"

"Not long I think. Everything is ready."

"What sort of business?"

"Just something which has to be tidied up."

The road to Ratisbon lay along the Swabian wall; a rough ditch and palisade of timber, with frequent log-built block-houses.

"Our British wall is of stone."

"This will be stone some day. The plans have all been made. They keep putting it off, first for one thing, then another, a raid here, a mutiny there, a corrupt slave-contractor, a commanding-officer too old for his job, always something more urgent to be done, never the time or the men or the money for anything except the immediate task. Sometimes I feel as though the Empire were like an unseaworthy boat; she springs a leak in one place, you caulk it up, bale out and then before you can settle down to navigation, water comes spurting in somewhere else."

Thus on some days, desponding, when they had found the post-horses galled and ill-fed or the guards shabbily turned-out; when at their halts they had fallen in with grumblers and rumour-mongers, with ugly, disloyal tales about the higher command; but, in general, Constantius's spirits rose as he rode daily deeper into the military zone; they travelled by easier stages now, unsaddled early in the afternoon, reported punctiliously at each Area Headquarters, talked at length and at ease to all they met.

For Helena, the scene, unchanging from morning to evening, was devoid of interest; the metalled highway, on one side vine and corn and cantonment, on the other the wild lands, untilled, wasted by generations of border fighting, burned-back as far as the eye could reach, naked of corn; between them the fosse and the ramparts; but Constantius was exhilarated; the siting of the guard-houses, the problems of water-supply and victualling, the varying amenities of the garrisons—a cockpit here, a rough sports stadium there, the greater or less propriety of the gaming-houses and taverns; the shrines of the regimental deities, the gossip in the mess about promotions and superannuations, new training methods, tricks to prolong the life of old weapons, tricks to get new issues from the supply dumps; all which stirred Constantius and led him to the very brink of enthusiasm, fell flat for Helena; even the stables, regularly laid-out, uniformly equipped, began to pall; only here and there on the road, when they met a party of haughty, naked Germans who had come over the lines to barter; now and then at the halts when the conversation turned upon wolves and bears, did her interest quicken. Once she said: "Must there always be a wall, Chlorus?"

"What do you mean?"

"Nothing really."

"I'm not a sentimental man," said Constantius, "but I love the wall. Think of it, mile upon mile, from snow to desert, a single great girdle round the civilized world; inside, peace, decency, the law, the altars of the gods, industry, the arts, order; outside, wild beasts and savages, forest and swamp, bloody mumbo-jumbo, men like wolf-packs; and along the wall the armed might of the Empire, sleepless, holding the line. Doesn't it make you see what The City means?"

"Yes," said Helena. "I suppose so."

"What d'you mean, then; must there always be a wall?"

"Nothing; only sometimes I wonder won't Rome ever go beyond the wall? into the wild lands? Beyond the Germans, beyond the Ethiopians, beyond the Picts, perhaps beyond the ocean there may be more people and still more, until, perhaps, you might travel through them all and find yourself back in The City again. Instead of the barbarian breaking-in, might The City one day break out?"

"You've been reading Virgil. That's what people thought in the days of the Divine Augustus. But it came to nothing; from time to time in the past we've pushed a bit further East, taken in another province or two. But it doesn't work. In fact we've lately had to clear out of the whole left bank of the Danube. The Goths are delighted and it saves us a lot of trouble. There seems to be a natural division in the human race just where the present wall runs; beyond it they're incurable barbarians. It takes all our time to hold the present line."

"I didn't mean that. I meant couldn't the wall be at the limits of the world and all men, civilized and barbarian, have a share in The City? Am I talking great nonsense?"

"Yes, dear child."

"Yes, I expect I am."

At length they reached Ratisbon, the largest town that Helena had ever seen; they stayed at Government House, the largest house Helena had ever entered.

"I must leave you here for a week or two," said Constantius. "You'll be in good hands."

The hands were those of the Governor's wife, a matron of Italy, of Milan, a patrician, half a head taller than Helena. She greeted her kindly.

"Constantius is a great friend," she said. "I hope you'll allow us to be friends of yours, too. You must get some clothes," she said. "You must get your hair and nails done. I can see Constantius has no idea of how to look after a bride.''

So a steward was sent off on the first morning into the market and returned with half a dozen merchants and a train of slaves and soon the drawing-room looked like a corner of the bazaar, with stuffs and ribbons spread everywhere, and all the senior officers' wives took a hand in fitting Helena out.

They sat in Helena's room while the barber did his work, commenting on the rare splendour of her hair as it mounted and rippled and took an alien shape under his hands.

"My dear, you bite your nails."

"Only lately; never before I left home."

No one asked her where she came from, and, obedient to Constantius, she was silent when the chance was delicately offered.

"She's going to be perfectly presentable," said the Governor's wife when the ladies were together after dinner, and Helena seemed out of hearing, absorbed in a puppy.

"Yes. Where do you think Constantius found her?"

The lady who spoke had married well, none knew whence. "I make a point of never enquiring into the origin of army wives," said the Governor's wife. "I am glad enough if they conduct themselves properly once they are married. Young men get stranded in the service for years at a time in most out-of-the-way places—without the chance of meeting girls of their own kind. One does not blame them if they sometimes marry rather oddly; one makes allowances and one tries to help."

When Constantius and she were alone that night, Helena said: "Chlorus, why don't you tell them who I am?"

"And who are you?"

"The daughter of Coel."

"They wouldn't be impressed," said Constantius. "You are my wife. That is all they need to know. What have you done to your hair?"

"Not me. It was the Greek barber. The Governor's wife made me have him. Don't you like it?"

"Not much."

"Neither do I, Chlorus; neither do I."

On the eve of Constantius's departure some functionaries from Moesia, old associates of his, dined at Government House and after dinner accompanied him to his quarters. Helena left them for bed but could hear them talking long into the night in the adjoining study, now in Latin, now in their own tongue, gossip, reminiscence. She dozed and woke to hear them still talking, in Latin now.

"We heard you had been all over the place in Gaul."

"No, no; just a routine tour as far as the Swabian wall."

"Well, you've got a girl who's unmistakably British, anyway."

"Nothing of the kind," said Constantius's voice. "As a matter of fact, if you must know, I picked her up last winter in the East, at a road-house on the way home from Persia. I couldn't bring her with me then so I arranged to have her sent to Trèves. I've just collected her."

"She doesn't look Asiatic."

"No, I've no idea where they got her from. She's a good girl."

Then they lapsed into their own tongue and Helena lay awake in the darkness. It was near cock-crow when Constantius bade them good-bye and came to bed.

Then he departed on his high and secret errand and Helena remained at Ratisbon. Summer broke deliciously along the banks of the Danube; Helena languished in halls too lofty for her and a company too numerous. None of the ladies of Ratisbon seemed ever to go out of doors except in curtained litters to pay calls from street to street or, rarely, to drive in closed carriages to one or other of the riverside villas. They talked endlessly in rapid, allusive Latin that seemed always to mean more to them than to Helena; they laughed endlessly at jokes she missed. There were two sets among the ladies of Ratisbon over whom the Governor's wife serenely and indifferently held sway—those concerned with love affairs, and the religious. Helena was no stranger to the laws of man's desire; at home she had watched her father's errant and exuberant fancies ring change after change in the precedence of his little household; in her reading she had followed all the crazy transmogrifications of desire, the incest, the cloud-kisses, the courting showers of coin, the swans and bulls, of ancient poetry; but here in the whispered confidences under the portico she found no part of her own steadfast and bruised passion. The religious, too, confounded her. In her own country the gods had been honoured in their seasons; Helena had prayed, year by year, devoutly and at her ease at the altars of her household and her people, had greeted the returning Spring with sacrifices, had sought to placate the powers of death, had honoured the sun and the earth and the fertile seed. But the religious ladies of Ratisbon spoke of secret meetings, passwords, initiations, trances and extraordinary sensations, of Asiatics who floated about the room in half-darkness, of enigmatic voices, of standing stark naked in a pit while a bull bled to death on the lattice above them.

"It's all bosh, isn't it?" she said to the Governor's wife.

"It's disgusting."

"Yes, but it's bosh, too, isn't it?"

"I never enquire," said the Governor's wife.

Esteem, almost affection, had grown in Helena's lonely heart for this great lady. To her, tremulously, she had confided the secret of her royal parentage, her Trojan descent. As Constantius had foretold, the Governor's wife was not impressed.

"Well, all that is over," she said, as though Helena had confessed to a peccadillo. "You must study to fit yourself to be Constantius's wife. You'll find that a whole-time job, you know. He's a very important young man. I sometimes wonder if you quite realize it. The Divine Aurelian thinks the world of him. What did you do all day in Britain?"

"I was being educated. I read poetry. I hunted."

"Well, you won't be able to do that now. No lady is supposed to hunt, though I did sometimes when we were quartered in Spain, I'm ashamed to say, and enjoyed myself enormously."

"Tell me about it."

"Certainly not. You'll never bear children if you hunt."

"I think I've got one now," said Helena.

"That's just as it should be, my dear. I hope it's a son. He may turn out to be someone of the Greatest Importance."

In all the exorbitant largeness of her circumstances nothing appalled Helena so much as these predictions. The Governor's wife was not the only one who frightened her in this way. A wealthy woman, whom blank plainness of mind and face excluded from both the religious and the smart sets of Ratisbon, was more explicit. From the moment they met she showed Helena marked attention; one day when Helena had refused to accompany her to a party she said: "I think you're quite wise to be a little stand-offish."

"Me," said Helena aghast, *"stand-offish."*

"Oh, Madame Flavius, I don't mean anything the least disagreeable. But you do keep people at a distance, don't you? And you're quite right. It's a great mistake in early life to tie yourself up with friends you may have to drop later."

"But why should I drop them? If you only knew how I long for a friend."

"Dear Madame Flavius, please don't pretend with me. I admire so much the way that you are carrying off the situation. Don't pretend you don't know you've made the most brilliant match."

"Yes, I know, but what's that got to do with dropping friends?"

"Is it possible, Madame Flavius, you haven't heard your husband is going to be given command of the whole West any day now? Don't tell me you didn't know."

"I didn't; truly I didn't. Pray God it's not true."

"But it's common knowledge. Everyone in Ratisbon is talking of it."

And it was suddenly borne in on Helena that those silences which fell when she entered the room, those glances she sometimes intercepted to see whether she was listening, were not, as she had supposed, due to her youth and foreignness, but to this more alarming cause.

It was as though she had fallen asleep in the secure, child's bedroom at Colchester—the low-raftered room that had been hers since first she slept alone, where sitting on the press she could toss her shirt to its peg on the opposite wall; where, dressing, she had countless times paced its length and breadth, two steps from press to looking-glass, four paces from glass to door—and had lived since in a nightmare where walls and ceiling constantly receded and everything but herself swelled to monstrous size and in all the remote corners dark shadows lurked.

Days and nights grew heavy with the heat; the ladies of Ratisbon plied ivory and feather fans, whispered and peeped, while Helena looked only for the return of Constantius.

He came at length early in August with the dust and stiffness of the road on him, and the lean look of the camp. There was a stir of deference and congratulation, for he was preceded, many days before, by reports of decisive action at Châlons, of the Army of Gaul destroyed and Tetricus in chains. He came in discreet triumph, full of the praises of Aurelian's generalship, silent on his own part in the business. Helena, for whom the Summer in vain had grown to fullness, welcomed him as the Spring.

"Everything went according to plan," he said. "Now for Nish."

They travelled by water, for Constantius became solicitous when he heard of her pregnancy, in a barge, a vessel of state, carved and painted, deep-laden with furniture and provisions from the rich markets of Ratisbon. The slaves pulled slow on their oars. Constantius was in no hurry now. He and Helena lay like princes of India under an awning of yellow silk; idly, daylong, they watched the rushy banks sweep by, threw sweetmeats to the naked urchins who swam to salute them, to the birds who followed their passage and perched sometimes on the gilded prow; at night they eschewed the towns and tied up on the bank at the leafy islets, lit a fire on shore and feasted the villagers who often gathered to dance and sing in its light. The guards and the boatmen slept ashore, leaving the whole splendid ship to be a marriage-bed for Helena and Constantius. Often in the morning, when they cast off, their guests of the night before came with garlands of flowers which died at midday and then were thrown overboard to drift more slowly behind them towards Nish.

Helena's love, sprung of the mists and rain, grew tender and Summer-sweet while the new life ripened imperceptibly within her; in those soft days of Constantius's holiday, her honeymoon deferred, Helena rejoiced to feel that she was loved.

They came to the whirlpool at Grein where, to humour Helena, Constantius ordered the helmsman to steer straight for the vortex of swirling, encumbered water; the leisurely slaves were caught unawares and the boat swung broadside across the stream; for a minute there was confusion on board, helmsman, master and pilot shouted to one another, the oarsmen awoke from their dreams of freedom and pulled furiously, and Helena laughed loud and clear as she used to laugh at Colchester. For a minute it seemed they were out of control and must spin helpless as the eddying driftwood about them; then order was restored, the boat was righted, drew clear, and resumed her course.

Presently they came to the sunless gorge of Semlin and there, awed by the vast precipices and momentarily recalled by them to the mood of Ratisbon, Helena said:

"Chlorus, is it true what they are saying in Ratisbon: that you are going to be Caesar?"

"Who say that?"

"The Governor's wife, the widow of a banker, all the ladies."

"It may be true. Aurelian and I have spoken of it before. After the battle he spoke of it again. He has to go to Syria now, to tidy up the trouble there.

After that he will return to Rome for his triumph. Then we shall see."

"Do you want it?"

"It's not that *I* want, ostler; it's what Aurelian wants that counts, he and the army and Empire. It's nothing to be shy of, just another, larger command —Gaul, the Rhine, Britain, possibly Spain. The Empire's too big for one man; that's been proved. And we need a secure succession, a second-in-command who's been trained to the job, knows the ropes, can step in straight away when the command falls vacant; not leave each army to declare for its own general and fight it out as they've done lately. Aurelian is going to talk to the senators about it when we go to Rome."

"O Chlorus, what will become of me then?"

"Of you? I haven't really thought, my dear. Most women would give their eyes to be Empress."

"Not me."

"No, I don't believe you would." He searched her with a long scrutiny. Her hair was still tiered in the height of fashion—a slave from Smyrna was attached to their party for this purpose alone; all that the dressmakers and kindred tradesmen could do, had been done to transform her; new beauties had been discovered, old beauties hidden, by their crafts; but as

Constantius gazed he felt bonds of the British spell still strong about him, he felt himself seduced from his cold intentions and transfixed anew as he had been that uncanny night in Coel's banqueting-hall.

"There's no need to worry yet, ostler," he said, "Aurelian's good for many more years."

But later she said: "Tell me about the battle. Were you in great danger? I never felt anxious about you while you were away. Should I have done?"

"There was no need. It was all arranged before-hand."

"Tell me."

"There was nothing to do on the day. Tetricus rode over with his staff and gave himself up. He had put his army just where we wanted them. All we had to do was wade in and cut them to pieces in our own time."

"Were many killed?"

"Not of ours, though the Gauls fought it out sur-prisingly well. There was nothing much else they could do. We had them surrounded."

"And Tetricus?"

"He'll be all right. We shall keep our bargain."

Helena asked no further questions. It was enough, in the sunshine, that Constantius was with her and complacent; but that night, when the golden canopy was black against the stars and the water lapped placidly on the sides of the boat; as the sentry ashore paced to and fro in the firelight and Constantius lay asleep, sated, as he had turned from her, as he always did, curtly without tenderness or gratitude, chilling her crescent ardour and leaving her lonely at his side as in the empty bedroom at Ratisbon; then, and often later at Nish when the leaves had fallen and the guards under the window stamped and chafed their hands in the first cold winds of winter—then the grim story haunted her. Something had died in her heart that had lived there from her earliest memories. Her nurse's father, that redoubtable sergeant, was dead, had died in vain, and his grave had been dishonoured. This was Chlorus's victory, this his mystery; for this his journey, his furtive interviews, his fox-like doubling on his tracks, his lies and silences; this butchery of a betrayed army, this traffic with the betrayer; this and herself were his joint prizes.

At length they reached the confluent Morava and, turning south, rowed upstream towards the mountains. As he approached his homeland Constantius grew impatient once more, forced the pace, stood for hours at the prow searching for familiar landmarks.

The men strained and sweated, the non-commissioned officers grew peremptory and Helena felt the chill of loneliness return to her heart.

They turned again from the main stream up another tributary; the hills closed in until one day at evening they reached the town that was to be Helena's new home. Officers, officials and a shabby crowd assembled to greet them. Since they left Strasbourg, Constantius had discarded the insignia of his assumed, modest rank; now before landing he donned the full finery of his command. All was not ready for their reception. Functionaries came on board and talked obsequiously while a carpet was spread on the rough wharf; the guard-of-honour marched up, resplendent but late; one sedan-chair and, after delay, a second, were set down between the rigid ranks. Only then, to a salute of trumpets, did Constantius lead Helena ashore.

Light was failing; the crowd pressed close, peering between the guards; Helena saw little of Nish on her way from the water-front. They went under an arch; through the windows of her chair and over the porters' shoulders Helena caught glimpses of an arcaded street, of the bases of many fluted columns, of a thronged square, and a line of over-sized, official statues; the scent of garlic and hot olive-oil,

pierced with a sweeter breeze from the mountains;
then she was set down and stepped from her close
cabin into the vast, paved square of the barracks,
bemusedly climbed the steps between ranks of
guardsmen and entered her house where the lamps
were already alight.

"I'm afraid you won't have thought much of the
turn-out," said Constantius.

"I noticed nothing wrong."

"They're a shocking lot of men—nothing but re-
cruits and the old sweats. Aurelian's been bleeding
us white, the last six months, for the army that's
forming for the Syrian campaign—draft after draft
of our best men, over ten thousand of them. He's
promised them back but you can never tell. There's
nothing but a token force now between here and
Trèves. We shall look pretty silly if the Goths
start anything. But they won't. They've had
something to remember too lately. If I have time
tomorrow I'll show you Uncle Claudius's battle-
field."

He showed her the battle-field in arduous detail,
the line where the legions had stood and broken
under the Gothic charge, the gully where Uncle
Claudius had cleverly concealed his reinforcements
and launched them on the enemy's rear, the foothills

where Uncle Claudius had rallied his shaken men,
turned them and led them back to victory, the open
fields where at length fifty thousand Goths had been
splendidly massacred. The salvage had been patiently collected and between the unconsidered
bones, the trampled vines, replanted, were even
now being picked. "Grapes thrive on blood," said
Constantius.

He showed her, also, the principal beauties of the
town, the statue of Uncle Claudius, seven and a half
tons of Pentelic marble with bronze enrichments; it
stood at the hub where all the roads of the province
converged and met the great highway that led from
the Rhine to the Euxine Sea; the more modest monument to Uncle Quintilius, a bust in the cooling-room
of the public baths; the massive shrine and domestic
altar of the Flavian family; the half-finished meat-
market Constantius himself had planned—work had
lagged there during his absence and was now furiously resumed; the court-house where he gave judg-
ment; the very chair he sat in on such occasions; his
box at the theatre.

Constantius was at home in Nish; here in his own
command, among his own people, his precise speech
betrayed the local burr, his manners at table became
rougher, he laughed, mirthlessly but from a kind of

contentment, at the jokes his subordinates made when they came to dine.

Various kin came to call from the surrounding hills; Helena often failed to follow their broken Latin. They commented coarsely on her now-evident pregnancy and, when these compliments were at an end, lapsed, with an air of physical ease, like a man unbuckling too tight a belt, into their mother tongue. Helena found none to love among them; they were a prosaic race; some farmed their ancestral holdings; some had profited by their high connexions to the extent of small trade monopolies and sinecures; many of them had not yet troubled to adopt the fanciful new patronymic of "Flavius."

The grapes were pressed, the leaf paled and fell, the first, premature snow melted as it touched ground; then after a few brumous weeks winter set in, hard and white, with cruel winds from the mountains. Helena patiently bore her growing burden, lay much indoors, borrowed the few rolls of poetry in the bank-manager's library, dreamed of Britain and the call of the hunting-horn in bare woods.

CHAPTER FOUR

The Career Open to Talent

Before midwinter news came from the East; first by courier in a brief, official notification of victory; shortly afterwards at great length over the plum-wine from one of the countless military cousins, a cocksure young centurion of infantry on special leave from the field.

"It all went according to plan. Trust Aurelian. Our boys did most of the fighting as usual."

"Did you see Zenobia?"

"Once, in the distance. She's something very special I can tell you. Aurelian's going to treat her soft, they say."

"Why?" said Constantius.

"If you ask me the old boy's breaking up a bit. He left Palmyra practically untouched. No massacre. No private looting. It didn't go down any too well with the troops. He chopped the block off an old boy called Longinus."

"Who was he?"

"Not the Great Longinus, the philosopher?" said Helena.

"Something of the kind. According to Zenobia he was behind the whole trouble. Why? Do you know anything about him?"

"I used to, once."

"I say," said the kinsman, "you seem to have introduced a highbrow into the family. We shall have to watch our steps."

"What can you possibly know about a philosopher?" asked Constantius Chlorus.

"Nothing much. Nothing at all really."

Yet the death of this remote old man, whose books she had never read, struck another wound in Helena's heart. He had joined the sapper-sergeant in the lost country of her British youth and it seemed that now, tragically, her education had come to its end:

"What about the triumph?" Chlorus was asking.

"That's all set as soon as the troops can be moved. It's a matter of transport. I wonder you aren't going. All the big shots will be there."

"I've heard nothing about it yet, officially."

"He's taking the whole army to Rome. I wish he wouldn't. The boys'll never be the same again."

"Odd I haven't been informed."

"Well someone has to stay behind and do the dirty

work I suppose. Besides, you weren't actually in the campaign, were you?"

"No. No, I suppose not. All the same, I thought Aurelian would want me there."

Constantius Chlorus fretted darkly for some days after this visit. Then the imperial courier arrived and his mood lightened; he was going to Rome. It was his first visit.

"Chlorus, I do wish I could go too."

"That's out of the question."

"Oh, yes, I know it's out of the question, but I've always so wanted to see a triumph."

"There'll be plenty more," said Constantius.

"You'll remember everything, won't you, every detail, and tell me about it when you come back?"

"There'll be a lot to remember if I know Aurelian."

Helena cried that evening and half-grudged the child in her womb its life and power to hold her imprisoned. She cried again bitterly when Constantius and his small escort rode away through the snow; then she composed herself and bided her time.

Her child was born in the new year. Constantius had left orders that it was to be called Constantia if it were a girl, Constantine if a boy. It was a boy; a robust baby acclaimed by all its father's kinswomen as notably handsome.

British mothers of the upper class followed the Gallic and Italian fashion and put their babies out to nurse; not so the Illyrians, as Constantius's relations unanimously sought to inform Helena. She complied joyfully with this primitive usage, suckled her boy, crooned to him and deeply loved him.

She lived in the promise of Constantius's return. So also did the cantonment and the neighbouring countryside. Almost every family had a man in the army; many of them veterans of the Gothic wars, whose term of service was up, who had been looking forward to discharge and a bonus of land, when they were drafted East; some were young soldiers, newly-married; the infant Constantine was one of a thousand babies in and about Nish whom their fathers had never seen.

Constantius returned with the Spring when the plain was white with plum blossom. A courier came first with orders for his reception and inquiries about his son. Crowds pressed round the man in the courtyard asking news of friends and kinsmen, but he rode back into the hills leaving them unanswered. A scare started in the garrison that something was amiss, that the army was being drafted East again, that there was plague in the column. No word of these rumours reached Helena. She nursed her baby, repeating over the cradle the message that in two days he would see his father.

When the day came she rode out to greet Constantius through the flowering orchards and vineyards, met him five miles up the road, turned and trotted home beside him. They spoke of Constantine and then he fell silent. Behind them, also silent, followed the vanguard of the Danubian army.

"Is anything wrong?" asked Helena.

"Yes. A misfortune. Nothing fatal. One of the things a soldier must expect."

"Tell me."

"Later."

And they rode silently into Nish.

The news, and more than the news in a hundred fantastic distortions, spread through the town. To correct the rumours Constantius issued a proclamation. The truth was grave enough. Part sullenly, part in Balkan gusts of grief, the townspeople pulled down the flowery arches with which they had decked the street, and gave themselves up to mourning. That evening alone with Helena, Constantius at last gave way to his grief.

"Seven thousand of my best troops, men who fought with Uncle Claudius, the bone and soul of the province, cut to pieces in the streets, in The

City . . . Some local grievance at the Mint, a towns-man's brawl . . . men who had fought three times their weight of Goths and Syrians, trapped and mur-dered in the slums by a rabble of slaves and circus hands . . ."

Bit by bit the grim story came out; the lax disci-pline after the triumph, the soldiers pushing their way happily about the markets, collecting souvenirs, seeing the sights, boasting in the taverns and baths; then the sudden, concerted uprising against them of half the city . . . "What's behind it? It wasn't a mere riot. They were armed and trained for the job, backed with money. What are they after? There's something we don't understand, working under-ground, planning . . . Some say it's the Jews. There are secret societies everywhere in Rome. You never know who you're talking to; the man next to you at dinner may be a member. Every class is mixed up in it. Women, too. Slaves and eunuchs and senators. They're out to destroy the Empire; God knows why. Aurelian says it's the Christians . . . It none of it makes any sense."

He spoke to Helena because she was his sole com-panion, but in his shame and perplexity he did not turn to her for comfort. He was not the man who had hopefully ridden out from Nish. In the days that followed, when the fatigue of the journey was forgotten and the first smart of loss dulled, and he was once more soberly and confidently calculating his chances of preferment, he was still a stranger to Helena. When he stood beside her as she nursed her baby, when he came to her bed, he was still a stranger. Rome, where all the treasure of the world flowed and was squandered, had despoiled Constantius. What he had ever had of youth was dried up now; whatever of love was all grown cold; that large shadow of him which Helena had glimpsed, pursued, briefly enjoyed, was lost forever. He was a man unschooled in courtesy; no inherited veil of kindliness hid his small, cold soul. Helena saw all this in the first days of his return and accepted it. Like the Spartan boy so often—so crassly it had seemed then—extolled to her in her childhood, she pressed the gnawing fox to her vitals and held him hid.

But because they were alone together evening after evening and his mind was shaken and clotted with the events at Rome, he talked long about them.

"The triumph was something I shall never forget, something I could never have imagined."

"Elephants?"

"Twenty of them and four tigers. Aurelian's

chariot had a four-in-hand of stags; there were ostriches and giraffes and animals there isn't a name
for, who've never been seen before. Zenobia came
down on hands and knees once from the sheer
weight of jewelry . . . Tetricus looking as pleased
as though it was *his* triumph in mustard-coloured
breeches . . . Sixteen hundred gladiators. You never
saw anything like it."

"No," said Helena, "never."

"We had parties every night. All the biggest senators opened their palaces to us. They're a queer lot.
One of them collected mechanical toys they make
for the harems in Persia. You couldn't understand
half they said. I felt sometimes they treated us as if
we were part of the wild animals from the procession, but they gave us some staggering dinners.
Everything was got up to look like something else,
partridges made of sugar, peaches of mincemeat;
you couldn't tell what you were eating. . . .

"The size of the place! You can stand on any of
the hills and look round and as far as you can see
there's nothing but roofs. Great blocks of flats six and
seven storeys high; and hardly a genuine Italian
in the place, every race and colour under the sun.
It shook the men, I can tell you."

And at the end inevitably the conversation came

back to its true course, Constantius's career: ... "For the first month I hardly saw Aurelian at all. He was with Probus all the time; a new man who's been lucky in the East. I began to think he was avoiding me. Then after the triumph was all over he called me in and we had a long talk. Everything's going to be all right. He's a great man, a second Trajan. He began by putting all the objections—the Senate were getting restive and thought we Illyrians were taking too much into our own hands; the army in the East didn't know me, and so on. I thought he was working up to say he'd changed his mind. Then he said: 'I'm telling you all this to show you your job isn't going to be easy.' No more than that but in his old quiet, friendly way. He had the proclamation made out for my appointment and another one outlawing the Christians. Then, if you please, a thunderbolt had to fall in his garden. He's a queer, superstitious fellow. He began consulting a lot of fortunetellers and put off signing anything. Then came that frightful rising in the city. After that he suddenly decided to go off to Persia. He says it's to get back the body of Valerian, but if you ask me he's afraid of the army. He's got to keep them on the move and in action for fear of mutiny. I hoped he'd take me with him. I tried to see him again and again. Then just when he was starting he sent me a message. I was to come back to Nish. I wasn't to worry. He had not forgotten me. So it's just a matter of waiting again. It won't be long this time."

But the Divine Aurelian never came back. He had barely started when he was murdered by his staff on the shores of the Bosphorus. News of the event came swiftly to Nish and was received with lamentation as general and bitter as for their own kin. Constantius was dumbfounded and made no move. The whole army seemed momentarily shaken in its self-confidence. No general put himself forward. Month succeeded month and the Empire lay inert, without an emperor. Then the Senate appointed one of themselves, a blameless elderly nobleman. There were no objections except from himself; he knew very well what it meant.

A few months passed and an Illyrian was again on the throne. Probus this time. Constantius patiently served, and advancing one lowly step in his ascent, when after a time as Governor to Dalmatia, while his rivals, Carus, Diocletian, Maximian, Galerius, clustered enviously round the seat of supreme power.

Constantine was just three years old when they moved to Dalmatia; sometimes for an hour or so he sat Helena's saddle astride before her; at other times he travelled on a led-horse, wrapped in furs, in a basket specially contrived for him. He slept long and seldom complained, watching the passing scene with silent interest. Because of the snow they followed the circuitous route up the Danube and Sava and across the mountains by the gentler, northern pass. On the edge of the high, blind plain of the Lika they re-ordered the caravan, transferring their baggage from the ponderous military wagons to the light, big-wheeled carts of the country, engaging a few guides and outriders and a local pioneer unit to go before them and clear the road.

Helena had left Nish without regret and she travelled forward without hope. They brought a sledge for her but she preferred to ride. Day by day they followed the brown ruts in the bland white surface. At the foot of the pass sledges were assembled from all the surrounding farms. The carts were driven up empty, left at the summit and the horses led back to drag the luggage, eight to a sledge with a dozen men about it, at the sides, at the back, at the horses' heads, pushing and pulling and shouting, till all the baggage was up. Then Constantius broke camp, breakfasted and saddled by torchlight, was off at the grey of dawn and rode through in the day to the first frontier town of his new dominion.

The joy of that day's ride took Helena unawares, so long had she ceased to look for it. All the morning they climbed; the baggage trains had worn the road bare and the horses stepped out firmly and bravely. The way ran zigzag through a forest of pine which the bitter wind, still that morning, had turned to ice; every bough was adorned with lines of stalactite which shivered and glittered in the morning sun; every needle had a brilliant, vitreous case and when she flicked her whip at a wayside shrub she brought down a tinkling shower of ice-leaves, each the veined impression of its crisp, green counter-part. The sun mounted with them and when, soon after noon, they reached the top of the pass and Constantius drew rein to inspect the loaded carts, Helena rode forward round a bare pinnacle of limestone, and came alone to an immense and splendid prospect.

The ice ended abruptly; six paces had borne her out of that soundless and scentless, lunar winter. Birds were in song all round her; the wooded hillside fell away, cleared and terraced on its lower slopes with vineyards and olive groves and orchards, while at its foot, far below, a river wandered through a rich landscape of villas and temples and little walled towns. Straight before her lay a primrose gleam of sunlit water, a line of purple and grey islands and beyond, above their crown, the single blue arc of the sea; and through the balmy smell of the woods her nostrils caught the distant, salt tang of the sea-side, of her first home. She had her child with her. "Look, Constantine," she cried, "the sea." And the child, sensing his mother's delight, clapped his hands and repeated, without meaning, "The sea. The sea."

The sun was in their faces now; with each step of the descent the air grew warmer and richer; half-way down Helena unbuttoned the short Dacian coat of bearskin she had worn during the journey, and joy-fully tossed it to the wagoners. That evening they stopped at the fort which held the foot of the pass and the people flocked round to greet them with jars of sweet wine and baskets of figs, sugared and packed layer by layer with bay-leaves. Next day they reached the sea.

Government House stood on a little creek, shel-tered from the open sea by a wooded islet dedicated to Poseidon. It was no new piece of official architec-ture but had been a summer palace of the old kings of Illyria and before that, tradition had it, the castle of Greek pirates; behind its new Vitruvian façade it climbed the hill in a series of irregular courts and arcaded gardens where the gardeners cutting back the clematis revealed marble capitals and plaques carved in the days of Praxiteles. Here Constantius justly and moderately governed his province. Uprooted from his homeland and estranged from his kin he assumed a manner that passed for dignity among his genial subjects. On all its frontiers the Empire was fiercely at war; Probus floundered round the periphery through sand and marsh slaughtering Sarmatians and Isaurians, Egyptians and Franks, Burgundians and Batavians; his grim chiefs-of-staff, Carus, Diocletian, Maximian and Galerius followed his eagles, watched him and counted their chances. Once or twice Constantius himself took the field in brief successful actions on the frontier. News of these victories came promptly to Dalmatia and was greeted with suitable official rejoicing. But there in that fertile and populous plain between the mountains and the sea, peace smiled; law was obeyed, the old gods were honoured, exquisite carpets were woven, private houses were fondly adorned, sweet must fermented, the oil ran in the limestone vats; there Constantine learned his letters, rode his first pony, practised the bow and sword; there Constantius took a mistress, a vicious woman from Drepanum ten years his senior, and seemed content.

And there, shy and impulsive, in sudden starts and pauses, as if playing with her affections the nursery game of "grandmother's steps," Helena made a friend, a widow who had retired there from the disorders of Rome, the benevolent mistress of a household as large as Helena's, a patron of local arts. To her, in time, Helena came to speak almost without reserve.

"It's odd," she said one day, "that Chlorus should have taken up with this woman. She doesn't look a bit kind. So much happens one never expected. I always knew that when I was old, he would want someone younger. Men always do. Papa did. I never expected him to give me up so soon, for someone nearly twice my age. I suppose that's what he wanted all the time really, never me. If only people knew what they wanted . . ."

"Helena, you're hardly grown up and you sometimes talk as though your life was over."

"It is really, at least all I used to think was life . . . like Helen's you know, at the fall of Troy."

"My dear, nowadays people marry again and again."

"Not me," said Helena. "Just at present I've got Constantine, but he'll grow up; then everything will be over; so much sooner than I ever thought."

"It's twenty years since I left Rome," said Helena's friend; "I haven't seen one of my old friends since; I have grand-children whose names I can't remember. I expect in Rome they all think of me as dead. Yet here I am well and cheerful, busy all day long, doing no one any harm and some people a little good, with the finest garden on the coast and a collection of bronzes. Don't you call that a full life?"

"No, Calpurnia, not really," said Helena.

Then for the first time in anyone's memory the Empire was at peace. Through the full length of its frontier the barbarians were stopped and shaken. Now for the first time there was a chance of restoration. Probus was the saviour of the civilized world. He turned his energies to the tasks of peace. A great undertaking was begun in the marshes of Sirmium. They were to be drained and planted and settled by his victorious and devoted veterans. Probus directed the work in person. One warm day the men got bored, chased the Emperor up a tower and murdered him on the summit.

When news of this incident reached Salona, Helena said: "That ought to make Chlorus a little happier about being on the shelf."

"Is he on the shelf?"

"Oh, yes, everyone has forgotten him now."

But this was not quite true. The new Emperor was Carus. He decided to attack the Persians, but before sailing he crossed the Adriatic and visited Constantius and talked to him at length, speaking the precise Latin of the Universities; a bald, leathery old soldier, but a gentleman.

"I served under your great-uncle Claudius," he said. "He gave me my first command. And I knew Aurelian well. He had great faith in you. They were great men, Claudius and Aurelian. We don't seem to get that type in the army any more. Somehow or other the mould got broken sixty years back. The young men—Galerius, Diocletian, Numerian—well, you know what they are like as well as I do. I can't abide the fellows. Do you know my boy, Carinus? I sometimes think he's wrong in the head. And do you know what I've had to do? Put Carinus in charge in Rome, simply because I can't find anyone better. That's a pretty state of affairs. He's doing no good there. I expect you've heard."

Constantius politely remarked that he had heard rumours, but disbelieved them.

"Whatever they're saying can't be much worse than the truth. He's made a pimp Consul and his hall-porter Governor of the City. He even employs a professional forger to sign his letters. Not that the Romans mind. They find it all very amusing. But it can't go on. As soon as I get back from Persia I shall put things straight. That's why I've come to you now. I'm giving you the West. You've done well here. You've done well wherever you've been. You're the man for the job. If things go too far in Rome and if anything happens to me, you're to step in at once and *act*. I know I can trust you."

Constantius Chlorus had heard it before. He heard it now with less exultation. But he was content. His time, long deferred, had come at last. He told Helena about it and she heard it with less than her usual despondency. It seemed not to matter, now, and, anyway, might not be true.

Next day Carus went back to his army.

Months passed. News came from East and West, of the steady advance and repeated victories of Carus, of the appalling profligacy of Carinus. Seleucia and Ctesiphone fell; the eagles were on the Tigris, were across and marching straight for Persia. Carinus had staged a battle between ostriches and alligators.

Then the familiar, paralyzing message. The Emperor was dead, burned in his tent, by an assassin, by a thunderbolt, none knew how. Carinus and

Numerian were being proclaimed everywhere.

And Constantius did nothing.

At this, his star-given opportunity, lethargy mysteriously fell on him. He went down the coast alone to a little villa he had there, and week after week received no messengers. Neither his wife nor his mistress had any word from him or any clue to what was going on in his mind.

When he came out of hiding it was all over. Numerian was dead; Apar, the Praetorian Prefect, was dead, murdered in open court by Diocletian, and the army was on the march home with Diocletian commanding it. Soon Carinus too was dead, stabbed by a cuckold Tribune, and slave-born Diocletian ruled the world.

For seven more years Constantius remained Governor of Dalmatia. Constantine had a tutor and a fencing-master and the games of childhood became the stern exercises of boyhood; he was quick to learn, handsome and affectionate. He wept to read of the death of Hector. "I *hate* Achilles, don't you, mummy. I hate all the Greeks. I do so wish the Trojans would win."

"Yes, I did, too, although Paris wasn't very nice, was he?"

"Oh, I don't know. He got what he wanted, any-way."

"So did Menelaus in the end."

"I wonder, do you think he still wanted her, mummy?"

He had his own boat and an attendant fisherman; together they sailed far out beyond the islands, re-turning at morning, when he would lurch into the dining-room at breakfast, rough-haired and rosy, and lay his dripping creel before his mother, proud as a dog with a rat. There was little of his father in the boy, save for occasional sullen moods when his small plans went awry; he yielded swiftly to Helena's teasing.

"You're a regular little Briton," Helena once said to him.

"You mustn't let father hear you say that."

"No, that wouldn't do."

"Father says I'm Illyrian and that is the race of the Emperors. I'm to be Emperor some day."

"Pray God not," said Helena.

"Don't you want me to be? Why not, mummy? Tell me. I won't say anything to father."

"The Emperor has all the enemies in the world against him."

"Well, why not? I'd settle them. Father says it's in my stars."

Helena reported the conversation later to her friend.

"He hasn't given up the idea, you see."

But Constantius no longer spoke what was in his mind. In that solitude, broken only by tidings of death, he had passed a climacteric; something had happened, an interior jolt and rearrangement, a twist of the kaleidoscope—such as he had experienced in Rome at Aurelian's triumph. (They were liable to sudden change, these "Flavians." Thus Constantine came to glory.)

Constantius lived alone now, save when he was with his troops. Helena passed days without hearing his voice. Quite alone; the Bithynian woman's palanquin was never again seen in the courtyard. One day Constantine came in from fishing, agog.

"Mummy, what d'you think we caught today? A body."

"Darling, how horrible."

"You can't think *how* horrible. It was a woman. She'd been in the water weeks, Mark said; her face was quite black and she was all blown-out like a wine-skin. And, mummy, she hadn't been drowned;

there was a cord, tight round her throat, sunk right in. I shouldn't have noticed it only Mark showed me."

"Darling, it was beastly of Mark and it's beastly of you to be so excited. You must try and forget it."

"Oh, I couldn't ever forget it."

And that night, when she came to kiss him good night, she found him bright and sleepless. "Mummy, Mark and I know who that woman was. It's father's lady. Mark could tell by a gold bracelet she had on. You could hardly see that either, the wrist was so swollen."

Constantius became faddy about his food; gave up beans and meat, and sometimes fasted all day. He rode often, sometimes twice a week, to his villa on the coast. But his work did not suffer. Whatever hours he kept, he was punctual in court, just and moderate; he never signed a paper unread; he emended the training reports of the army, he studied the accounts.

"What does he do at that house down the coast?" asked Helena. "I suppose he's got another nasty old woman."

"It sounds to me, my dear, as though he had got religion."

It was the truth, the simple explanation of

Constantius's new life, of his aversion from beans, of the inflated horror bobbing at the end of the fish-line.

Many years before, as a subaltern, Constantius had been initiated into the cult of Mithras. There were a number of odd regimental ceremonies to which newly-joined officers submitted; he accepted this as one of them. The occasion made no deep impression. He was led by the adjutant through the by-ways of the garrison town to an unobtrusive door. He was blindfolded, his hands bound in warm, wet gut; he was led down steps into a place that was hushed and warm. There he took an oath inviting extreme penalties if he ever disclosed what was now to be told him. He was then told a Secret. He repeated it, as he had done the oath, word by word after his director. It had no meaning for him—a string of uncouth Persian vocables, the names, he was told later, of seven lesser devils, henchmen of Ahriman; special names by whose use they could be placated. Then the bandage was removed and he saw a lamp-lit vault, the bas-relief of a bull-fight, and, in his immediate proximity, the familiar, friendly faces of half the mess. While he was with his regiment he attended off and on, saw other men initiated as he had been, heard talk of higher degrees of enlightenment and of deeper secrets. Then he had been taken up, moved about, isolated, and he had thought no more about these fraternal gatherings.

He was not twenty then. His way seemed straight and plain as a trunk-road. He asked no guide or prop on the journey before him. Now, nearing middle-age, scant of hair, lonely, unregarded, with his passions turning sour within him, trapped and caught as though in a dream by the gladiator's net, frost-bound in his own private, perpetual winter, he reverted to the occult aid offered him in his free youth.

There was a cave near his villa, which was well known as a place of the Mysteries. The land for some acres round it was enclosed in a wall and left uncultivated save for a small vegetable plot behind the parsonage; a path, unpaved, led through stone-pine and boulder to a cave's mouth at the edge of the sea. Here, on certain nights of the month, the hooded devotees resorted, drawn from barracks and warehouses, men of all degrees, unknown to one another elsewhere; and dispersed again silently after the rites of their various businesses.

One day during the interregnum, while Constantius paced and sprawled in the agonies of indecision, the priest came to call at the villa, hoping for a subscription. Constantius received him with suitable condescension.

"I was a Raven once at Nicomedia, father."

"I know." It was his business to know just that kind of thing. "How long is it since you came to the Mysteries?"

"It must be seventeen years; more, eighteen."

"And now, I think, you are ready to return."

The priest had assumed authority; they were no longer Governor-General and subject but instead pupil and catechist, penitent and confessor. The priest spoke in abstruse, allegorical terms of matters Constantius had never considered; much of what he said was meaningless, but through it all ran a single intelligible thread. Light, Release, Purification; a Way Out.

Day after day the priest came to the villa. Presently Constantius joined the congregation in the cave. He fasted and bathed; he accepted the veil of Cryphius and the Soldier's brand. And there he stopped short. The priest urged him to prepare for the honey and ashes. "You are merely on the threshold. All you have done so far is mere preparation. You are still far out in the darkness. Beyond the Lion is the Persian, beyond him the Courtier of the Sun, beyond that the Father; so much I know;

but beyond that is still another degree of which we do not speak, of which I know only the outer vestige, where there is no matter, no darkness, only Light and the ineffable One.''

"These things are not for me, father."

"They are for all who seek."

"I am content."

Constantius had found what he wanted, the thing without which his talents availed him nothing; he did not ask more.

He attended the cave regularly. He persisted in his single prayer, for release, for purification, for power through freedom and purity. There was a draper admitted as Soldier on the same night as himself who at the first rhythmic incantations invariably grew stiff, stood with pop eyes and grinding teeth, twisted spasmodically in fierce convulsions and uttered harsh, wordless cries. This man speedily rose to higher planes and no longer appeared at the same meetings as Constantius. Many outdistanced him in the race for enlightenment. Constantius was not competing; he drew strength month by month, year by year, from the divine toreador for the simple, earthly task he had set himself.

When Constantine was fourteen years old his father took him to the Mithraum.

"Did you enjoy it, darling?" Helena asked on his return.

"We don't speak of these things to women, do we, father?" her son answered.

"What do they *do?*" she asked Calpurnia later.

"My dear, I think they dress up. Men love that. And they act sort of plays to each other and sing hymns and have the usual sacrifices, you know."

"Why do they make such a secret of it?"

"That's half the attraction. There's no harm in it."

"I hope not. It all sounds very odd to me. Constantine has come home saying he is a Raven."

She pressed her husband for information. "There's no harm in your knowing the general story," he said. "It's very beautiful," and he told her the tale of Mithras. He told it rather well and she listened intently.

When it was finished she said, "Where?"

"Where?"

"Yes, *where* did it happen? You say the bull hid in a cave and then the world was created out of his blood. Well, where was the cave when there was no earth?"

"That's a very childish question."

"Is it? And *when* did this happen? How do you know, if no one was there? And if the bull was the first thought of Ormazd and he had to be killed in order to make the earth, why didn't Ormazd just think of the earth straight away? And if the earth is evil, why did Mithras kill the bull at all?"

"I'm sorry I told you, if you simply wish to be irreverent."

"I'm only asking. What I want to know is, do you really believe all this? Believe, I mean, that Mithras killed his bull in the same way you believe Uncle Claudius beat the Goths?"

"I see it's no good talking to you about it."

So Constantius went his pale way, seeking neither plain truth nor ecstasy, subduing the cloying powers of darkness by continence and a diet of eggs, and Constantine grew to gallant manhood and Helena by imperceptible stages and without regret lost her youth.

Diocletian had divided the Empire with Maximian, left him the embattled frontiers of the West, and spun himself intricate cocoons of court-etiquette at Nicomedia. At length Constantius was summoned there.

For the last year he had been grim and calm, expectant. It was as though a long gestation complicated in its early stages by alarms and whims was at last coming healthily to birth.

"This is undoubtedly something of great importance," he said when he received the Emperor's despatch.

"Yes," said Helena sadly, "another move."

"I look forward to seeing all the changes at Nicomedia. He's entirely modernized the place. They call it the new Rome," he said.

"Do they?" said Helena sadly. It seemed a name of ill omen.

He was soon back, resplendently, imperially overdressed.

"Chlorus, the purple!"

His was not the complexion for it.

"Yes, at last."

"You always meant to have it, didn't you?"

"It has been a long time coming and now it's all happened so quickly and quietly that I can hardly believe it's true. You'd never believe the way Diocletian lives. People used sometimes to say that Aurelian rather overdid things. They should just see Diocletian in full court rig. You have to go in on all fours and kiss his skirts. I never saw anyone look so shy in my life as old Maximian holding a gold pineapple in a suit so stiff with gold lace and jewels he could hardly move. We had to stand behind Diocletian for two or three hours while more and more fellows came crawling in—officials and ambassadors—all with speeches they'd obviously been preparing for weeks beforehand. I couldn't believe they were meant seriously at first—fantastic, flowery stuff. I don't suppose Diocletian understood a word. He just stood there looking stuffed—like Valerian. Then when it was all over he called the three of us, Maximian, Galerius and me, into his office. You should have seen the change. He took off his coat, sat down in his shirt sleeves and said, 'Orders, gentlemen,' just as he used at a staff conference in the field. He had it all worked out to the last button. We had nothing to do but agree. He and Maximian have both adopted a Caesar, me in the West, Galerius in the East. We become emperors automatically after them. There are to be no more disputed successions . . . So much waiting and hoping and now, when it happens, it's as simple as promoting a new centurion." He sat in his purple cloak entranced by the mystery of success. "There were times, ostler, I thought it would never come off." He used the old, fond nickname without design, a fruit of his happiness.

"I'm very glad for you, dear. When do we move?"

"Oh," he said, "there's one part of the plan I haven't told you. I've married again."

Helena sat, struck dumb. Constantius paused, then as she said nothing continued affably: "You mustn't mind. There's nothing personal in it. Galerius had a wife, too, he's had to divorce—a girl he was very fond of. Diocletian had the divorce papers already made out for us to sign; all perfectly legal and above board, you know. I've married Maximian's daughter, Theodora. I don't know what she's like—haven't seen her yet. She's meeting me at Trèves."

Helena still said nothing. They sat in silence apart, each with separate thoughts; how far apart appeared when Constantius next spoke. "If it had happened any sooner or in any other way, I might now be dead," he said reverently.

At length Helena said: "And has Diocletian decided what's to happen to me?"

"To you? Why, anything you like. I should marry, if I were you, and settle somewhere."

"Then please, can I go back to Britain with Constantine?"

"That's impossible. There's a very nasty little rebellion in Britain at the moment. Besides, I'm sending the boy away directly."

"Sending him away? Where?"

"To Nicomedia. It's time he started his political education."

"Could I go with him?"

"No, that wouldn't do. But go anywhere else. You've the whole Empire to choose from. Look, they're lighting a bonfire. How very touching. It's quite spontaneous, you know."

On Poseidon's island, opposite the palace, an orange light rose and spread; the guards had built a pyre there since the first advanced-riders had brought the news of Constantius's elevation. Helena had watched them at work that afternoon, wondering idly what they were about. A crowd stood in plain outline feeding the flames and other boatloads, singing, were even now being ferried across from the dark shore into the firelight. The first, resinous smoke drifted to the terrace where Helena and Constantius sat. Pine branch and myrtle kindled and crackled; soon the big timber caught and the flames streamed skyward, yellow at the roots, red and full-billowing, folding under and over in the pungent smoke, hidden, breaking out in small tongues and a spray of sparks.

The household servants ran out on the lower terrace, to the sea's edge, clapping and laughing; the men on the island cheered; more boats put out from the mainland.

"What did you say?" said Constantius.

"Nothing, I was talking to myself."

"I thought you said something about Troy burning."

"Did I? I don't know. Perhaps I did."

"A highly unsuitable comparison," said Constantius Chlorus.

CHAPTER FIVE

The Post of Honour
Is a Private Station

FOR thirteen years Helena lived alone. Her hair lost its fierce colour and, scorning dyes, she wore it always wound in a silk shawl. She thickened in limb and body, held herself firmer, moved more resolutely, spoke with authority and decision, took careful count of her possessions, gave orders and saw them obeyed. She had moved, on Constantius's elevation, from Government House to his villa, purchased and enclosed a large estate and made it thrive. She knew every man and beast on the place and the yield of each plantation; her wine commanded a high price in the market at Salona. Westward in the rough seaface of the sheltering islands the great waves struck and splattered; eastward in winter, the high Dinaric forests were torn by blizzards which the people of the plain never heard; nor saw save as a smudge of indigo on the mountain crests and in the wreckage which drifted on the tideless channel and lay there, barely stirring, for the boys to pick. Here among oleander and myrtle, lizard and cicada, Helena gently laid down the load of her womanhood. Here, it seemed, far from home, she would in full time die.

Constantius reigned sedately in Gaul. Constantine followed the fortunes of Galerius and the Eastern army. Beastly Maximian bullied the Italians and the Africans. The work of empire prospered, frontiers were everywhere restored and extended, treasure accumulated. But, out of sight on the shores of the Propontis, where the vested chamberlains stood like dummies, motionless as the stuffed thing that had hung in the Persian court, and the eunuchs scuttled like pismires when a soldier passed them; in the inmost cell of the foetid termitary of power, Diocletian was consumed by huge boredom and sickly turned towards his childhood's home.

He ordained a house of refuge on the shores of the Adriatic. Labour was impressed all over the province, a hillside was stripped of its timber, supply-ships rode in the bay. Walls grew at a startling pace.

Helena and Calpurnia spoke of the new palace as "the eyesore." Once when it was nearly complete, they drove round to inspect. It was the size of a garrison town; the neighbouring farms had been emptied and their fields rutted and trodden to waste. It stood in a new, raw desert of its own making. Masons' dust, trodden to paste in recent rains, clogged their feet, as they followed the clerk-of-the-works through the vaulted tunnels and blind caverns of new-cut stone. They plodded for an hour through the whitish mud. They were shown the cranes, the concrete mixers, the system of central heating, all of the latest pattern. Around them and above their heads gangs toiled on ropes and windlasses, dragging the great blocks on ramps and rollers, swinging them into place; skilled artisans astride the scaffolding were chipping out, hour by hour, yard by yard, the regular scrolls of ornament. The two made suitable comments on the scale and efficiency of the work, took gracious leave and when they were alone in the carriage looked at one another with consternation.

"It's not a style that would ever go down in Britain," said Helena at length.

"I suppose it's very modern, dear."

"Not a window in the whole place."

"On our lovely coast."

"I never met Diocletian. My husband had a great respect for him, but I don't think he can be very nice."

"The coast will never be the same again if he comes to live here."

"Perhaps he'll never come. Emperors often don't do what they want."

But he came before he was expected, before the palace was furnished; without music, a legion of silent, tramping men, a litter in their midst; secretaries and doctors trotting round the litter; all disappeared into the new palace like gnomes into the cleft rock in a story Helena's nurse used to tell her years ago in Colchester. Rumour said the Emperor was dying in agony; then after six months the procession emerged and swung East on the road to Nicomedia. He would return, rumour said; the Dalmatians watched and listened and remained glum.

"I think I shall leave," said Calpurnia. "I could never feel happy with that creature squatting so near. Let's go together to Italy."

"I shall never move now. The time for that is past. I wanted to travel once, to Troy and Rome. After that I only wanted to go home to Britain. Now I've struck root here, emperors or no emperors."

"They say Constantius is going to be Emperor of the West. That's why Diocletian has gone to Nicomedia. He and Maximian are retiring."

"Poor Chlorus," said Helena. "He's had to wait a long time. He must be quite an old soldier now. I hope he's still able to enjoy it. He did want it so."

"It will make a difference to Constantine."

"I pray not. If only Constantine can keep clear

of politics, I sometimes hope that perhaps one day, when he's finished his service, he may want to come and settle down here with me. He's married now with a son. I've made the place very nice for them. Just right for a retired colonel. If only he keeps clear of politics."

"That's a lot to ask of an emperor's son."

"Oh, Chlorus has his own political wife and plenty of political children. Constantine and I are private."

She heard from Constantine regularly in dutiful, solicitous letters from Egypt and Syria and Persia and Armenia; she received frequent exotic gifts. His portrait, by a Greek, hung in her bedroom. Report made him an athlete, a serious soldier, a favourite in camp and at court. Any ex-serviceman from the East found hospitality at her house and a reward for news of him. Of Minervina, his wife, she learned little. "I suppose Chlorus didn't write much about me," she reflected. The grandson had been named Crispus, a family name among the "Flavians." "I think he might forget the Moesian connexion," she said.

"Perhaps he's proud of it," said Calpurnia.

"He couldn't be. Such dull, pushful people."

"They're the nearest thing we have to a royal family, Helena."

"Oh, he must forget that too."

She bought more land, though prices were rising all along the coast since Diocletian had begun to build there. She started draining operations on some barren salt-marsh. "He's used to big undertakings," she explained. "He will want to keep busy." She planted rows of tiny olive plants, a special Spanish type slow of growth but heavy of yield. "Perhaps, before they fruit, Constantine will be here," she said. He was the focus of all her plans.

At length after thirteen years, quite suddenly, he came and all her plans were at once obliterated.

He came at sunset. "We're off at dawn," he said. "You too, mother."

He was just as she had imagined him, the portrait in full life, large, loving and rather formidable.

"My dear boy, I couldn't possibly go anywhere at the moment."

"I'll explain later. I must look after horses while the light holds. Minervina is outside with the boy. You might see if they need anything."

First things first; Helena went to the hall where she found, hunched on a marble seat, as she had been left, an almost insensible young woman and a small boy.

"My dear, I am Constantine's mother. I am afraid you are tired out."

Minervina began to weep.

"Mother's always tired," said the child; "I am always hungry." He was strolling about confidently and curiously. "I'm not a bit sleepy," he said.

The servants were bringing in the saddle-bags.

"Would you like something to eat now?" Helena asked her daughter-in-law, "or a bath before dinner?"

"Nothing to eat. I just want to lie down."

Helena led her to a room. A maid tried to help, but as soon as Minervina's boots were off she lay back on the bed, rolled to face the wall and immediately fell asleep. Helena looked at her a moment and then led Crispus from the room.

"We've had such a ride," he said. "Father had all the post-horses hamstrung behind us. Last night we never went to bed at all. We just lay down for a bit on straw at one of the inns."

"Let's see if we can find some supper. I am your grandmother."

"My grandfather is Emperor. Are you an empress?"

"No."

"Then you can't be my *real* grandmother, can you?

Father says I had another grandfather, but he wasn't real either. Can we go down to the sea?"

"Tomorrow perhaps."

"Tomorrow we have to ride on again. I'm going to be a sailor when I'm Emperor."

"Do you want to be an emperor, Crispus?"

"Of course. There's two sorts of emperor you see, bad and good. The bad Emperor is trying to stop us getting to the good Emperor, my grandfather. But he won't. We've been too quick for him and we've done for his horses."

"Things are breaking up," said Constantine after dinner. "They just held together as long as Diocletian was there. Now there'll be trouble everywhere. You must come to my father's territory."

"My dear boy, who is going to worry about a woman like me, living my quiet private life here?"

"You don't understand modern politics, mamma. There are no private lives nowadays. You are my mother. That will be enough for Galerius."

"And you are a Tribune in Galerius's army. You ought to be with your men, not careering across the Balkans laming a lot of good horses."

"I have no choice. When the historians write of

me they will say that if I wish to live, I must determine to rule."

"Oh, *history*. I've read quite a lot sitting alone here year by year. Keep out of history, Constantine. Stay and see what I have done, the clearing and draining and planting. That is something better than history. And if I go, it will all fall to waste."

"Mamma, the whole Empire is going to waste. For the last century we have hung on by bluff and luck. People seem to think the Empire is eternal. They sit at home, read Virgil, and suppose everything will go on just as it always has done, without any effort on anyone's part. On the frontier I have seen a whole province run to waste in a season.

"I've been haunted lately by a vision of what might one day happen if we cease to fight—a dusty world, with all the canals of Africa and Mesopotamia dried up and the aqueducts of Europe breached, a line of broken arches here and there in a dead world divided between a thousand squabbling barbarian chiefs."

"And so you are off to join forces under the Divine Maximian," said Helena. "That, I suppose, will save the world?"

" '*Divine*,' " said Constantine. "Does anyone, do

you suppose, really believe Maximian is a god? Does anyone believe in any of the gods, Augustus even, or Apollo?"

"So many gods," said Helena, falling in with her son's mood; "more every day. No one could believe in them *all.*"

"Do you know what holds the world together? Not the gods, nor the law nor the army. Simply a name. The fusty old superstitious sanctity of the name of Rome—a bluff two hundred years out of date."

"I don't like to hear you talk like that, Constantine."

"Of course you don't. Thank God there are still millions of old-fashioned people like yourself who feel slightly uncomfortable when Rome is mentioned. That is what holds the world together—a slightly uncomfortable feeling. No one feels like that about Milan or Nicomedia, though politically they're the important places nowadays. That is sanctity. If only we could make Rome really holy again . . . Instead we have the Christians. You should have seen some of the evidence that came out in the trials at Nicomedia. Do you know what *they* call Rome? 'The Mother of Harlots.' I've seen it in their books."

"But surely they've all been put down now?"

"It's too late. They're everywhere. The army and civil service are rotten with them. You can't disperse them as Titus did the Jews. They are a complete State within the State with their own laws and officials. My father hasn't even tried to enforce the edict in his territory. I'm told half his court are mixed up with them. They have their holy places in Rome itself—the tombs of their first leaders. They've their own Emperor, or something like it, living in Rome at this moment, giving his orders. They're the biggest single problem in the whole Empire."

Constantine fell silent and stretched himself wearily. "You'll start with us tomorrow, mamma?"

"Not tomorrow. I can't leave all these people here so suddenly. They expect more of me than that. I wasn't brought up in your kind of court, my son. Besides, I doubt whether I should be welcome at your father's. Go ahead, find some little place for me in the North. I'll follow you," and then she added: "These Christians—I wonder if in their way they too look on Rome as a holy city."

"My dear mother, I've told you. Their books . . ."

"Oh *books*," said Helena.

CHAPTER SIX
Ancien Régime

An Indian ape, the recent expensive present of a visiting diplomat, rattled his gold chain on the terrace. Helena threw him a plum. "I remember my late husband," she said, "once telling me that there would never again be another disputed succession. This year we have six Emperors. That's a record I think. They've even taken to calling *me* Empress."

"Not me," said Minervina.

"No, my dear, but I daresay they will in time. It is no good moping, least of all about a thing like that. I was divorced, too, you know, precisely as you have been. It upset me at the time but I assure you I have had a far happier and safer life as the result. It's only politics. I daresay Constantine regrets the change just as much as you do. I am told Fausta's an odious girl, surrounded by Christians. And anyway, you have Crispus. They took my boy away, you know. You should interest yourself in the garden. I should very much like to know what's happening to mine. With all these Emperors about, travel is quite out of the question. If they would only stop fighting, I should like to go back to Dalmatia. Not that I don't find this place quite enchanting."

For the third summer they were at Igal, two hours' drive from Trèves. Constantine had left them there on his road to power, not entirely forgotten, for Minervina had received her divorce papers and Helena the letters-patent proclaiming her Empress Dowager, at about the same time. Once, briefly and rather overwhelmingly, Constantine had dropped in to see them and had enlivened the occasion by slaughtering an entire army of unarmed Franks in the theatre.

The place was well-chosen, better perhaps for a lady of Helena's years than for Minervina. When you had seen the prodigious marble statue of Jupiter, the iron Mercury and the painted Cupid, you had seen everything that attracted the tourist. But these works were truly remarkable. The Cupid, crucified by women, drew tears. The Mercury was poised in full flight between two loadstones. The Jupiter held a golden thurible, two feet across, like a toy in his marble fingers, and grains of incense thrown into it filled the whole temple with sweetness while remaining unconsumed and undiminished. "Of course it's all a trick," said Helena. "But I can't think how it's done and I never get tired of seeing them do it."

And besides these fabulous treasures Trèves had many delicate charms; its gardens ran down to the Moselle, ran up into the hills; the water-gates were gold-starred and surmounted by five great crowns. It was an enchanting place, with all the opulence and chic of Milan sharpened by a Northern tang of its own which Helena recognized and loved.

There was a Celtic air, too, which was still dearer to her. Poets abounded. "I don't think they mean a great deal," Helena said in answer to Minervina's peevish questions, "but they are thoroughly nice young men and very badly off; they like coming here and when they read aloud they do so much remind me of my dear father in one of his poetic moods."

Minervina yawned in Helena's salon. It was not what she was used to in the Middle East. Lactantius shunned it. This celebrated man was ostensibly Crispus's tutor, but lessons had never prospered and soon lapsed. It was all of a piece with Constantine's vague conception of splendour to search out from obscurity the greatest living prose stylist and set him to teach the obstreperous little prince his letters. Crispus now played all day long with boats and catapults and lorded it over his contemporaries, while

Lactantius followed his own calling in his own quarters. He appeared on demand when Helena wished to make a show of him, and sometimes at his own fancy when he would pay a call on the ladies, as he was doing that afternoon, to remind them, if they seemed to forget it, of his continued existence at their court. He had outgrown ambition but he believed that it would not be convenient to be entirely forgotten.

The post suited him well, for he was a Christian; he had got out of Nicomedia only just in time. Half his friends were caught in the latest wave of arrests and executions. Others of them turned up in Trèves from time to time with horrible stories. Refugees naturally headed there for it was one of the safest towns in the Empire, with a Bishop and countless priests going openly about their business. One was not starved of the sacraments in Trèves. What irked Lactantius was the lack of a theological library. The Bishop was an admirable man but his books were negligible. Lactantius had been able to bring nothing with him save his own manuscripts and was thus left, with all his unrivalled powers of expression, rather vague about what to express; with, more than that, the ever-present fear of falling into error. He delighted in writing, in the joinery and embellish-

ment of his sentences, in the consciousness of high
rare virtue when every word had been used in its
purest and most precise sense, in the kitten games
of syntax and rhetoric. Words could do anything
except generate their own meaning. "If only I were
a little braver," Lactantius sometimes thought, "if
I had dared stay nearer the centre of things, across
the Alps, I might have been a great writer."

The Christians were not the only cult that flour-
ished in the mild air of Trèves; the city—Eastern in
this respect, rather than Northern—teemed with
mystagogues of one sort and another, and Minervina,
who formed a taste for such company in the
Middle East, had a coterie of them, which Helena
deplored. Almost everything about Minervina was
objectionable but Helena bore with her for the sake
of Crispus, now eleven years old, who in his grandmother's fond eyes daily relived the brave childhood
of Constantine.

It was to Gnostic friends that Minervina now re-
ferred when she said: "I shall be glad when we move
back to town. I miss my Souls."

"You have quite a little colony of your persuasion
here in Igal, I think, Lactantius."

"Three families for whom your Majesty very kindly
found cottages when they arrived from Thrace. A

priest visits them; I, too, sometimes. They seem happy enough though it is a strange country for them; and they are simple people who speak no Latin."

"It's funny, nowadays, how much talk there is everywhere about Christians. I don't remember ever hearing of them when I was a girl in Britain."

"We have our martyrs there too—before your imperial husband's day of course. We are very proud of Alban."

Minervina fidgeted in disapproval and said: "I daresay the whole thing is very much exaggerated. I expect it will all blow over."

"It must be a sad time for your people," said Helena.

"Also a very glorious time."

"Really, Lactantius, what possible glory can there be in getting into the hands of the police?" said Minervina. "I never heard such affectation. If you feel like that I wonder you didn't stay at home in Nicomedia. Plenty of glory there."

"It needs a special quality to be a martyr—just as it needs a special quality to be a writer. Mine is the humbler rôle, but one must not think it quite valueless. One might combine two proverbs and say: 'Art is long and will prevail.' You see it is equally possible to give the right form to the wrong thing, and the wrong form to the right thing. Suppose that in years to come, when the Church's troubles seem to be over, there should come an apostate of my own trade, a false historian, with the mind of Cicero or Tacitus and the soul of an animal," and he nodded towards the gibbon who fretted his golden chain and chattered for fruit. "A man like that might make it his business to write down the martyrs and excuse the persecutors. He might be refuted again and again but what he wrote would remain in people's minds when the refutations were quite forgotten. That is what style does—it has the Egyptian secret of the embalmers. It is not to be despised."

"Lactantius, dear, don't be so serious. No one despises you. We were only joking. I should certainly never permit you to return East. You're a great pet and everyone here is very fond of you."

"Your Majesty is too kind."

With the first chill of autumn the household cumbrously removed to Trèves, advance party, main body, rear body, as in a military manoeuvre, ensuring the greatest possible delay in the brief journey. Minervina found the town, or rather her particular set there, agog with the prospect of a visit from a Gnostic of the highest distinction. He came from Marseilles with a great reputation bustling on in advance. He was quite the latest thing in Higher Thought. "I won't have him here," said Helena. "And that's flat."

"I don't suppose he would want to come," said Minervina. "He doesn't at all like grand life, I am sure. I expect he will have a little cell in the house of one of the Souls. They go for weeks without eating or sleeping, you know."

But when at last the savant arrived he did not eschew the hospitality of the second best house in Trèves. "You'll come and hear him speak, won't you?" said Minervina, and at length, because despite her placid habit of life and her decisive manner, she was troubled always with the suspicion that there was still something to be sought which she had not yet found, Helena consented.

When the day came Helena, as her position demanded, was last to arrive. Her hostess met her on the steps and led her to the hall which was full of ladies—not only the mystical set but the entire high society of Trèves—and led her to a chair, placed by her direction, at one side. The lecturer was already in his place. He bowed to the Empress and his hostess in a manner that suggested familiarity with the best society, and began.

Helena made some small business with her shawls which were not needed. The room was centrally heated and intensely hot. She discarded the lamb's wool and took a light Asiatic silk, creating all the time a little disturbance of ladies-in-waiting and slaves about her chair; then she surveyed her immediate neighbours, nodded affably to some of them, then folded her hands and turned her attention towards the lecturer.

He was an elderly, fleshy man, sagely bearded with the simple robes and practised manner of a professional philosopher; his dark, questing eyes moved among the audience in search of sympathy, found Helena's and briefly held them. He was at that moment employing her name and gave it, she thought, a slight inflexion of recognition.

. . . "Sophia," he was saying, "who, as Astarte, abandoned her flesh in Tyre, and as Helena was the partner of Simon, the Standing One; she, of many forms, who is the last and darkest of the thirty Aeons of light and by her presumptuous love became mother of the seven material rulers . . ." The tones were fruity and curiously familiar. They carried Helena back to a windy tower long ago, almost forgotten.

"It's him all right," thought Helena. "There's no mistaking him; Marcias, still up to his old tricks."

All round her the idle ladies sat in their various ways absorbed. One or two had their tablets with them but they took few notes. Helena saw that her lady-in-waiting had twice scratched the single word "Demiurge," and twice ploughed it through. Those who still sought to follow Marcias's meaning, looked anxious; happier those who surrendered without resistance to the flood of buoyant speech and floated supine and agape; they were getting what they had come for. Helena studied the row of blank profiles. She looked at Minervina who sat facing them at the lecturer's side. At the close of each paragraph Minervina nodded, as though confirmed in an opinion she had long held.

"All things are double one against another," said Marcias and Minervina nodded. "So the things of error come; then the Gnosis intervenes. Dosithus knew himself not to be the Standing One, acknowledged his error, and in his knowledge was made one with the mensural twenty-nine, and with Helena, the thirtieth half-one" ("Not this Helena," thought Helena)—"who is both mother and bride of Adam the primal."

Minervina nodded, deeply and gravely into the

roll of firm flesh below her chin, and Helena felt something shockingly unsuitable to the occasion take shape deep within herself and irresistibly rise; something native to her, inalienable, long overlaid, foreign to her position, to marriage and motherhood, to the cares of her great household, the olive-presses and the almond picking; foreign to the schooling of thirty years, to the puzzled, matronly heads in the stuffy, steamy hall; something that smacked of the sea-mist and the stables and the salty tangles of a young red head. Helena fought it. She compressed herself in the chair, she bit her thumbs, she drew her scarf over her face, she ground her heel against her ankle-bone, she tried furiously to cram her mind with all the sad things she knew—Minervina's Bithynian accent and deserted Dido—but without avail. Overborne, all the more audible for her efforts at suppression, Helena began to giggle.

The infection did not spread. The lady-in-waiting with the wax tablet recalled from aberration by the clucking at her side and observing Helena's veiled face and trembling shoulders, supposed that something pathetic had been said, scented tears, and not to be outdone in delicacy of feeling, assumed her own particular expression of woe.

The voice rippled on, and when Helena at length

had hold of herself, was at the peroration. The hostess said her words of thanks: ". . . I am sure we are all a great deal clearer than we were on this important topic . . . the lecturer has kindly consented to answer any questions . . ."

No one spoke immediately; then: "I was not quite sure whether you said that the Demiurge was an Aeon."

"No, madam. It was one of the aims of my poor discourse to demonstrate that he was not."

"Oh . . . thank you."

Minervina nodded as though to say: "I could have told you that, and I should have done so rather more sharply."

There was a further pause; then in clear, school-room tone, Helena said: "What I should like to know is: When and where did all this happen? And how do you know?"

Minervina frowned. Marcias replied: "These things are beyond time and space. Their truth is integral to their proposition and by nature transcends material proof."

"Then, please, how do you know?"

"By a lifetime of patient and humble study, your Majesty."

"But study of what?"

"That, I fear, would take a lifetime to particularize."

A little murmur of admiration greeted this neat reply and on the crest of it the hostess rose to dismiss the meeting. The ladies rustled forward towards the lecturer but he, deprecating their flattery, came to greet Helena. "I was told your Majesty might do me the honour of coming."

"I scarcely hoped you had recognized me. I am afraid the lecture was far above my head. But I am delighted to see you have prospered. Are you . . . are you able to travel as you wish?"

"Yes, I was given my freedom many years ago by a kind, foolish old woman who took a fancy for my verses."

"Did you get to Alexandria?"

"Not yet, but I found what I wanted. Did you reach Troy, highness?"

"No, oh no."

"Or Rome?"

"Not even there."

"But you found what you wanted?"

"I have accepted what I found. Is that the same?"

"For most people. I think you wanted more."

"Once. Now I am past my youth."

"But your question just now. 'When? Where? How do you know?'—was a child's question."

"That is why your religion would never do for me, Marcias. If I ever found a teacher it would have to be one who called little children to him."

"That, alas, is not the spirit of the time. We live in a very old world today. We know too much. We should have to forget everything and be born again to answer your questions."

Other ladies, eager to be presented to Marcias, stood round him, keeping their distance until the royal interview was ended. Helena surrendered him to them and was led to her litter. Minervina remained to wallow in the new revelation.

That evening Helena sent for Lactantius and said: "I went to the lecture this afternoon. I found I knew the man quite well. He used to belong to my father in Britain. He's put on a lot of weight since then. I couldn't understand a word he said. It's all bosh, isn't it?"

"All complete bosh, your Majesty."

"So I supposed. Just wanted to make sure. Tell me, Lactantius, this god of yours. If I asked you when and where he could be seen, what would you say?"

"I should say that as a man he died two hundred

and seventy-eight years ago in the town now called Aelia Capitolina in Palestine."

"Well, that's a straight answer anyway. How do you know?"

"We have the accounts written by witnesses. Besides that there is the living memory of the Church. We have knowledge handed down from father to son, invisible places marked by memory—the cave where he was born, the tomb where his body was laid, the grave of Peter. One day all these things will be made public. Now they are kept a secret. If you want to visit the holy places you must find the right man. He can tell you, so many paces to the East from such and such a stone, where the shadow falls at sunrise on such and such a day. A few families know these things and they see to it that their children learn the instructions. One day when the Church is free and open there will be no need for such devices."

"Well, that's all most interesting. Thank you, Lactantius. Good night."

"Good night, your Majesty."

"No one has seen him for nearly three hundred years?"

"Some have seen him. The martyrs see him now."

"Have you?"

"No."

"Do you know anyone who has?"

"Your Majesty, I must beg you to excuse me. There are things that must not be spoken of to anyone outside the household."

"I should not have asked. All my life I have caused offence to religious people by asking questions. Good night, Lactantius."

"Good night, your Majesty."

CHAPTER SEVEN

The Second Spring

FOUR years passed. Crispus was called to his father's headquarters and left jubilantly. Minervina married an ambitious, bald young Belgian and lost interest in the Higher Thought. The Indian ape aged prematurely, took sick in the chill river-mist and died. In his own time, the ripe and right time, Constantine marched into Italy.

Rumour and courier arrived simultaneously from Rome. Trèves was agog; all save the Empress Dowager. Her life had abounded in such tidings; one victory more, one emperor the less, another family pact between the victors, another loveless marriage; she had seen it all time and again; the division of spheres of influence; the start of another brief period of plotting and spying; these things came and went in their eccentric orbits.

The Edict of Milan, giving toleration to the Church, was promulgated at Trèves.

"Why all the excitement?" said Helena. "No one has interfered with the Christians here since my

126

husband's day. For weeks you have been going about as if you had seen a vision, Lactantius. You, a historian who thinks in centuries?"

"As a historian, ma'am, I think we are living in a unique age. This little battle at the Milvian Bridge may one day count with Thermopylae and Actium."

"Because of the Praetorians? I can't help being rather sorry for them, you know, even though they were on the wrong side. I never saw them on parade. It was one of the things I used to look forward to."

"The Praetorian Guard has had no importance, ma'am, for a hundred years."

"I'm only teasing, Lactantius. Of course I know why you are all so excited. I confess I am a little uneasy myself, It's this story that's going round that my boy has turned Christian. Has he?"

"Not exactly, ma'am, as far as we can learn. But he has put himself under the protection of Christ."

"Why will no one ever talk plain sense to me? Am I too stupid? It is all I have ever asked, all my life, a straight answer to a straight question; and I never get one. Was there a cross in the sky? Did my son see it? How did it get there? If it *was* there and he saw it, how did he know what it meant? I don't profess to know much about omens but I cannot conceive of a more obvious sign of disaster. All I want is the simple truth. Why don't you answer me?"

After a pause Lactantius said: "Perhaps because I have read too much. I'm not the person to come to with straight, simple questions, ma'am. I don't know the answers. There are those who do, the sort of people who stayed behind in the East. They will be coming out of prison now, what's left of them. They'll be able to answer you, but I doubt even their being quite as straight and simple as you want. All I can say is: it may have happened just as the people say. Such things do happen. We all have the chance to choose the Truth and I daresay emperors sometimes have the chance offered them in a more spectacular way than humbler folk. All we know is that the Emperor is behaving as though he had seen a vision. As you know, he has brought the Church into the open."

"Besides Jupiter and Isis and the Phrygian Venus."

"Christianity is not that sort of religion, ma'am. It cannot share anything with anybody. Whenever it is free, it will conquer."

"Perhaps there was some point in the persecutions then."

"The blood of the martyrs is the seed of the Church."

"You get it both ways, then."

"Both ways. We have that promise, ma'am."

"It is always the same, Lactantius, when we talk about religion. You never quite answer my questions but you always leave me with the feeling that somehow the answer was there all the time if we had only taken a little more trouble to find it. It all seems to make sense up to a point, and again beyond that point. And yet one can't pass the point . . . Well, I am an old woman, too old to change now."

But in that unique Springtide there was no escape from change, not even in Trèves, most polite of cities, not even for Helena, most secluded of women. The huge boredom which from its dead centre in Diocletian's heart had soddened and demented the world, had passed like the plague. New green life was pricking and unfolding and entwining everywhere among the masonry and the ruts. In that dawn, reflected Lactantius, to be old was very heaven; to have lived in a Hope which defied reason; which existed, rather, only in the reason and in the affections, quite unattached to common experience or calculation; to see that Hope take substantial and homely form near at hand and on all sides, as a fog, lifting, may suddenly reveal to a ship's company that, through no skill of theirs, they have silently drifted into safe anchorage; to catch a glimpse of simple unity in a life that had seemed all vicissitude—this, thought Lactantius, was something to match the exuberance of Pentecost; something indeed in which Christmas, Easter and Pentecost had their royal celebration.

He, if anyone, should have understood what was going on round him, but he was left breathless, quite outrun, with all his fine vocabulary exhausted and only the clichés of court eulogy ready to mind. Events were no longer following their humdrum human pace. There was a disproportion everywhere between cause and effect, between motive and movement, an intervening impetus and increase beyond normal calculation. In his dream a man may put his horse at a sizeable obstacle and without design, take wing and soar far above it, or seek to move a rock and find it weightless in his hands. Lactantius had never learned to subdue his sympathies as the critics prescribed. What was left to him now but to accept the mystery and glorify the proximate cause, the distant, ambiguous Emperor?

In terms of documented history Constantine had done little. In most of the West the Edict of Milan merely regularized the existing practice; in the East it comprised a precarious truce, swiftly repudiated. The Supreme Deity recognized by Constantine was something far wide of the Christian Trinity; the Labarum a highly heraldic rendering of the cross of the martyrs. It was all very vague, very plainly designed to please; the lucky thought of a man too busy to worry about niceties or profundities. Constantine had made terms with a new ally of unknown strength; he had shelved a problem. So it might seem to the strategists of the East who counted the order of battle, legion by legion, granary by granary; so, perhaps, it seemed to Constantine. But as the news spread everywhere in Christendom, from every altar a great wind of prayer gathered and mounted, lifted the whole squat smoky dome of the Ancient World, swept it off and up like the thatch of a stable, and threw open the calm and brilliant prospect of measureless space.

The oblivious Caesars fought on. They marched across frontiers, made treaties and broke them, decreed marriages and divorces and legitimizations, murdered their prisoners, betrayed their allies, deserted their dead and dying armies, boasted and despaired, fell on their swords or sued for mercy. All the tiny mechanism of Power regularly revolved, like a watch still ticking on the wrist of a dead man.

Far behind the fighting the royal women beguiled the time with their eunuchs and chaplains; they ac-

quired engaging young clergymen from Africa, well
bred, well read, who taught all manner of variations
of the orthodox creed. One week they talked of
Donatus; of Arius the next.

Everywhere Constantine prospered until he became blandly aware that he was invincible. Here
and there amid the chop and push of the times there
were glimpses of a nobler figure; young Crispus, all
dash and fidelity, last warrior of the high Roman
tradition on whose shield the fanciful might descry
the fading blazon of Hector. Reports of him came
to Helena, as once of his father, and were as fondly
welcomed. His name was remembered always at
her palace Mass. For Helena had been baptized.

None knows when or where. No record was made.
Nothing was built or founded. There was no public
holiday. Privately and humbly, like thousands of
others, she stepped down into the font and emerged
a new woman. Were there regrets for her earlier
loyalty? Was she persuaded point by point? Did
she merely conform to the prevailing fashion, lie open
unresisting to Divine Grace and so without design
become its brimming vehicle? We do not know. She
was one seed in a vast germination.

Surely, now, she needed all the last years left to
her to grow undisturbed? The strong, questing will

had found its object; the exile her home. The Empire was united and at peace. The Faith was established. All that remained for the Dowager Empress was to nestle down in her cradle of universal respect and prepare her soul for the day when she would find herself wafted to heaven and royally received there.

Those who spoke thus did not know the new Helena. She was past seventy when Constantine invited her to his jubilee celebrations at Rome. And off she went at once for her first visit.

CHAPTER EIGHT

Constantine's Great Treat

No one had really expected the Empress Dowager to come to the Jubilee. The invitation had been sent as a matter of form. The acceptance caused perturbation among the chamberlains. None of them had ever seen her but one thing was certain; there were far too many women about the court already. There was the Empress Fausta, always a troublemaker. It had been a bad day when Constantine gave the Lateran Palace to the Pope and moved her with all her children to the Palatine. There was Constantia, the Emperor's half-sister, the widow of Licinius; her presence and her son's was a continual, painful reminder of the circumstances of his death. There were Anastasia and Eutropia and the wives of Julius Constantius and Dalmatius, four ladies who set problems of precedence. There was no room at the Palatine Palace for the Empress Helena.

After much discussion they hit on the Sessorian Palace, a splendid old house with a large garden, on the walls, near the Theatre Royal. The neighbourhood was slummy but it was not to be expected that a woman of her years would go out much. The chamberlains set to work filling it with valuable furniture.

To reach this dower-house from the Flaminian Gate Helena had to cross the whole of Rome, up the Corso, under the slope of the Capitol, through the Forum, past the Colosseum, out through the old walls to the Celian hill, through the arches of the Claudian aqueduct, at last to her grand and lonely lodging. The way was cleared for her on her first arrival but everywhere from balconies and side streets rose the hum and chatter of a million and a half Romans, and everywhere behind the façades of the temples and the historic buildings of the Republic stood the huge, new, shabby apartment houses, island-blocks ten storeys high made of rubble and timber, sub-let and sub-divided, tottering with the weight of humanity.

It was Spring and everywhere fountains were playing among the falling smuts. But Rome was not beautiful. Compared with Trèves it seemed gross and haphazard. Beauty would come later. For centuries the spoils of the world had flowed into The City, piled up and lost themselves there. For centuries to come they would be dispersed and disfigured. The City would be burned and pillaged and deserted, and the marble stripped for the kiln. The streets would silt up, gypsies would bivouac under her broken arches, and goats pick their path between thorn and fallen statuary. Then Beauty would come. She was on the way, far distant still, saddling under the paling stars for the huge journey of more than a thousand years. Beauty would come in her own time, capricious, adorable wanderer, and briefly make her home on the seven hills.

Meanwhile there was the mob. Not on her first arrival in the curtained litter, but later when, contrary to expectation, she tirelessly followed the tourists' round, Helena daily saw more men and women than ever before in the total sum of her lifetime.

The Romans emerged at first dawn filling the streets and seeming to live there until sundown. After dark came the carriers' carts and farm wagons rolling to market by torchlight all the night through. The City was always overcrowded but now for the Jubilee there was added a huge press of officials and sightseers, hucksters and crooks, paying anything for a roof, sleeping anywhere; a motley lot, grasping and pushing and peering everywhere, Levantines, Berbers, blacks, amid the etiolated and stunted progeny of the slums. A few years earlier Helena would have shrunk from them, would have had a posse of guards whacking and barging to clear a little cloister for her to move and breathe in. "Odi profanum volgus et arceo." That was an echo from the old empty world. There was no hate in her now and nothing round her was quite profane. She could not dispense with her guard but she mitigated their roughness, and always her heart was beyond them, over their big shoulders, in the crowd. When she heard Mass at the Lateran basilica—as she often did in preference to her private chapel—she went without ostentation and stood simply in the congregation. She was in Rome as a pilgrim and she was surrounded by friends. There was no way of telling them. There was nothing in their faces. A Thracian or a Teuton might stop a fellow countryman in the streets, embrace him and speak of home in his own language. Not so Helena and the Christians. The intimate family circle of which she was a member bore no mark of kinship. The barrow-man grilling his garlic sausages in the gutter, the fuller behind his reeking public pots, the lawyer or the lawyer's clerk, might each and all be one with the Empress Dowager in the Mystical Body. And the abounding heathen might in any hour become one with them. There was no mob, only a vast multitude of souls, clothed in a vast variety of body, milling about in the Holy City, in the See of Peter.

Helena had not travelled light. A great caravan preceded her, a great household accompanied her on the road. More stores, more furniture and a second complete household awaited her at the Sessorian Palace. It took some time to settle in and, meanwhile, before order was properly established, visitors began to arrive.

Constantine did not come himself. He sent the Lord Chamberlain to greet her outside the gates. He sent a daily message of enquiry and duty. He expressed the hope of calling on her as soon as she was composed after her journey. But he did not come. Nor did Crispus. Nor did Pope Sylvester who was a near neighbour. She sent the Pope gifts. He sent a blessing but remained at home. It was not a very easy time for him. If he emerged he would have to take part in the celebrations, and it was never quite certain beforehand whether Constantine's celebrations would be Christian or pagan. Augurs cropped up. There was no recognized protocol for the treatment of an unbaptized convert—one indeed who was not yet formally admitted as a catechumen—who was at the same time a stupendous benefactor, an amateur of theology and the pagan Pontifex Maximus. Moreover, preposterous and highly embarrassing rumours were going about that Sylvester had recently cured the Emperor of leprosy. So the Pope pleaded ill-health and stayed at home conferring with his architects about the new basilicas.

The Empress Fausta was the first to call. She came indeed all too early, on the very evening of Helena's arrival, laden with fragile, expensive gifts, her eyes bulging with curiosity. It was not her habit to consider the convenience of others. Her mother-in-law might be weary from the journey, the house might be in disorder, but Fausta intended to be there first, to size up the old lady.

Helena greeted her rather distantly. There were many stories in circulation about Fausta's moral character, but stories of that kind did not reach Helena. She saw her, rather, as the symbol of something even more unlovely; an epitome of the high politics of the age.

Fausta's grandfather had been a nameless illiterate; her father, the odious Maximian. It was for an older sister of hers that Constantius had divorced Helena. For Fausta Constantine had divorced Minervina. There had been one motive only in that marriage, to solemnize the friendship of Constantine with her father and her brother Maxentius. Maximian he had strangled at Marseilles; Maxentius, a little later, he drowned in the Tiber. And somehow out of all that ritual of peace-making there survived one relic, this fat common little woman, Empress of the world; like a doll floating on the water where a ship had foundered.

She stood a full head shorter than Helena and dimpled when she smiled. Left alone she would have been unremarkably plain, but the beauty specialists had been to work on her. She glittered and pouted, "like a great gold-fish," Helena thought. But Fausta smiled, unconscious of the impression she gave. She was determined to be agreeable. She had her vices and her plans. At the moment she had a mission. The craze was theology and things had not gone well for her protégés in theological circles. The Empress Dowager might be a valuable ally. It was essential to put the whole question to her in the right light, before anyone else got at her.

"Sylvester?" she said with a wave of her plump white hand. "Oh yes, of course you'll have to meet him. It's only polite. And of course we all respect his office. But he's not a man of any *personal* distinction, I assure you. If he's ever declared a saint they ought to commemorate him on the last day of the year. A thoroughly holy, simple old man. No one has a word against him except that, frankly, between ourselves, he is something of a bore. I'm all for holiness, of course. Everyone is now. But after all, one is human. I'm sure in Heaven, when we're all holy, I shall be very pleased to spend hours on end with Sylvester. Here on earth one does want a little something besides, don't you think? Now take the Eusebiuses. They're some sort of cousin and absolute pets, both of them. I mean you feel they are one of *us*. I've got Nicomedia with me here. He's under a sort of cloud and has to keep away from his diocese for the time being. Such luck for us. I'll bring him round to see you. Caesarea couldn't come. He's the literary one and terribly busy. They're both very much upset at the moment. You see everything went wrong last year at Nicaea. It was terribly important. I don't exactly know why. Sylvester isn't interested in that sort of thing. He didn't even trouble to go himself, just sent deputies, and they were no help. You see none of the Western bishops have got a new idea in their heads. They just say: 'This is the faith we were taught. It is what's always been taught. And that's that.' I mean they don't realize they've got to move with the times. It's no use trying to puncture the horologium. The Church isn't a hole and corner thing any more. It's the official imperial religion. What they were taught may have been all very well in the catacombs, but now we have to deal with a much more sophisticated type of mind altogether. I don't pretend to understand what it's all about but I know the Council was a great disappointment even to Gracchus."

"Gracchus?"

"My dear, we always call *Him* Gracchus. Security, you know. Walls have ears. One can't be too careful after that last silly proclamation positively encouraging informers. It just isn't done to use His name. It makes everyone feel so awkward. Of course you and I could, but one gets out of the habit.

"Well, you know what Gracchus's Greek is like. He can get along all right giving orders and all that kind of thing—garrison Greek as they call it—but when the professional rhetoricians get going, the poor boy is quite lost. He hadn't the least idea what was going on at Nicaea. All he wanted was a unanimous vote. Well, half the Council wouldn't argue and wouldn't listen. Eusebius told me all about it. He said the moment he saw them sitting there he realized it wasn't worth reasoning with them. 'That's the faith we've been taught,' they said. 'But it doesn't make sense,' said Arius. 'A son *must* be younger than his father.' 'It's a mystery,' said the orthodox, perfectly satisfied, as if that explained everything. And then there was the Resistance Group. Of course everyone admires them tremendously. It's wonderful what they went through. But, I mean, just having an eye out and a foot off doesn't qualify one in theology, does it? And of course Gracchus being a soldier had a sort of extra respect for the Resistance. So what with them, and the solid Middle-West and the frontier bishops—there weren't many of *them* but they are the most pig-headed of the lot—the stupid old diehards won hands down and Gracchus got his unanimous vote and went off happy. Only now he realizes that nothing has really been settled at all. A General Council was just the worst way to tackle a problem of this kind. It ought to have been settled quietly in the Palace and then announced in an Imperial decree. Then no one could have objected. As it is we shall have all sorts of technical difficulties in putting things right. All that invoking of the Holy Ghost put things on the wrong footing. It was purely a question of practical convenience to be settled by Gracchus. I mean, we must have Progress. Homoiousion is definitely dated. *Everyone* who really counts is for Homoousion—or is it the other way round?

If Eusebius were here he would tell us. He always makes everything so clear. Theology's terribly exciting but a little muddling. Sometimes I almost feel nostalgic for the old taurobolium, don't you?"

The Empress Fausta was accustomed to talk freely and without fear of contradiction. Eusebius often told her that she had a man's mind in her grasp of a problem. But now as she drew to the close of her briefing she became aware that all was not quite well. The Empress Helena was regarding her with a look of thunderous disapproval.

After an awful pause, Helena asked: "And how is Crispus?"

"We always speak of him as 'Tarquin.' "

"Indeed. Pray do not let me influence you in the matter. I prefer to call my son and grandson by their own names."

"Well, you'll find it makes people very shy. Anyway, Tarquin is *not* much talked about at the moment. I think he's in some kind of trouble."

"That sounds most unlikely."

"Well, don't quote me. I never enquire into such things. All I know is, that he is *not much talked about*. Such a shame. He's really a very fetching boy."

"I shall call at the Palatine shortly and satisfy myself."

"Yes, do. I don't know quite who you'll find. Gracchus isn't seeing anyone at the moment. He's in one of his moods. My dear, I haven't even set eyes on him myself since that terrible day of the Knights Procession. But of course *I* shall be very pleased to see you. I'd like to show you my bath. Gracchus had it put in for me when I moved from the Lateran. It really is something very special. Every minute I spend anywhere else seems pure waste of time. I could die there quite happily. In fact, to tell you the truth, I ought to be there now. If I don't get my two hours every afternoon I'm fit for nothing at dinner."

When Helena went to her room that night she found something nasty, a little roll of paper, on her pillow which read: *Fausta is an adulteress.*

She burned it in disgust and had all the household woken and questioned. None could explain its presence.

It did not readily occur to the Empress Fausta that she made a bad impression. She came again next day bringing with her Eusebius, the celebrated Bishop of Nicomedia. "Marcias writ large," thought Helena the moment she saw him. He had fine dark eyes and a beautiful voice. He knew just how to treat great ladies.

"And how is our friend Lactantius?" he asked. "Tell me, ma'am, what did you make of his *Deaths of the Persecutors?* I confess I wasn't quite happy about it. There were parts which, really, I could hardly believe he wrote. A kind of brusqueness. I can't help thinking it was a mistake his going to live in the West."

"There are many excellent young poets at Trèves," said Helena.

"Of course, of course, and I know how much they owe to your Majesty's patronage. But, I wonder, are young poets *quite* the sort of company Lactantius needs? These earnest young backwoodsmen have a richness of imagination, a feeling for nature, a sense of the primitive virtues which we all applaud, but surely a writer of Lactantius's character should live in the heart of things."

"Do you feel in the heart of things here, Bishop? Do you find the Romans backwoodsmen?"

Eusebius gave her the sweet and quizzical glance that won all hearts,—or nearly all; not Helena's. "Your Majesty is very direct. Is that a fair question to put to a simple clergyman? Of course, wherever the Emperor holds court *is* the heart of things but—may I be direct too?—one does hear talk of a Great Move, does one not?"

"Does one?"

"Let me put it this way. Rome has a past. Rome *is* the past. But what of the future? Is it too rash to hint that perhaps in a few hundred years it will be laughable to speak of it as the centre of Christendom? A great commercial centre, no doubt. The primatial see still, possibly. I daresay as a mere matter of ceremony the Bishop of Rome will always take first place. But when we consider the great lamps of Christian civilization, where in the future will we look? to Antioch, Alexandria, Carthage."

"Nicomedia and Caesarea," said Fausta.

"Perhaps even to those humble sees also, ma'am. But certainly not to Rome. Romans can never be Christian. The old religion is deep in their blood. It's part of their whole social life. Of course there have been plenty of conversions in the last ten years, but who are they? Almost all Levantines. The solid core of The City, the knights and senators, the genuine Italians, are all heathen at heart. They're just waiting till the Emperor goes, to restart the old shows in the Colosseum. They say they're glad to see the Christians getting fat. That is why it sometimes seems rather a pity to be spending all this money here on building these enormous churches. What do you think?"

Only once did he touch directly on theology. "I don't suppose you are much troubled by controversy at Trèves." he said.

"We are conservative there."

"Well, ma'am, it is a highly specialized question."

"And the specialists have lately decided for conservatism; yourself, too, I believe."

"Yes, yes, we all voted dutifully with the majority. It is not an occasion to remember with pride. I said to our impetuous Egyptian friend as we came away: 'Better men fared thus before you.' I can't say it seemed to comfort him very much; yet after all what is a majority? A wave of irrational sentiment, a lump of unconsidered prejudices. Human reason survives such rebuffs. What happened to Troy? It seemed impregnable and a few men and a wooden horse brought it down. The forts of folly will fall in the same way. No, I am not greatly impressed by the Priams and Hectors of Nicaea."

That evening Helena found a message under her window: *Eusebius is a heretical Arianizer.*

"My correspondent has certainly got something

there," she thought. "I wonder if he was right about Fausta."

On another day Constantia came with her son Licinianus, a glum, shifty boy, rising twelve. His life, like a Greek drama, had been full of great happenings off-stage while a chorus of nurses, aunts and tutors held him perpetually bemused. Once he had had a resplendent papa who moved in and out of his small world to the sound of trumpets. And then had fallen a great silence in which his papa's name was never mentioned in his presence again. Now he lived under the same gilded roof as the most alarming of all his family, the highly-scented lady who bewilderingly was both aunt and great-aunt to him and seemed thus the heiress of a double portion of malevolence; often when he looked up from his listless games, he caught Aunt Fausta's terrible fish-eyes on him with an expression which loosed all his muscles and made him wet the floor. Nothing interested this little boy; it was as though he were here on such a short visit, in such a strange land, that it was really not worth while trying to understand anything.

"So you've met our darling Bishop," said Constantia. "Do tell me what you thought of him."

"Creepy-crawly."

"Oh."

"What is the matter with the boy? Why can't he keep still?"

"He's a little nervous."

"Of me?"

"No, no. He is always nervous. I'm sure I don't know why."

"You should take him away to somewhere healthy."

"Oh, we couldn't leave Gracchus. He's been so kind to us. The moment our backs were turned people would start saying things about us. You don't know what they're like. And I couldn't bear to have Gracchus think anything nasty about us. But I expect the whole court will go East again soon. I do hope so. I don't like Rome, do you?"

"It's not quite what I expected."

"I don't feel the Romans really appreciate Gracchus. There was that shocking affair the other afternoon when the Knights had their procession. Tell me are these your own slaves?"

"I brought them with me, most of them."

"Then I suppose it's all right to speak freely."

But she spoke with great caution. Every subject, domestic or public, seemed to crawl with possible misunderstanding. Presently Constantia rose to go.

"Tell Crispus to come and see me," said Helena.

Constantia winced. "Tarquin? Yes, I will, certainly, if I see him."

"Why should you not see him? He's at the Palatine, isn't he?"

"Yes, but it's so large, so much ceremony, so many different establishments. Sometimes one goes days without seeing anyone."

That evening the message which Helena had come to expect, folded this time in the crack of her door, read: *Beware of the conspirator Licinianus.*

All the royal ladies called. Word had gone round that Helena was indeed someone to be reckoned with. Often she was out sightseeing, often she was in church; but in the course of the first ten days the whole doomed Flavian family managed to meet her. By each she sent a message to Crispus and at last he came, unheralded, after dark. He threw himself into his grandmother's arms and when he stood back he was weeping.

They talked late. Twice in that night he thought he heard movements on the terrace outside and had the garden searched by linkmen. Once he threw open the door suddenly but found in the passage only a faithful old maid from Gaul who was trimming the lamps.

"It seems to me you have all worked yourselves up into an extraordinary state of nerves on the Palatine," said Helena. "The whole lot of you. You're just like that wretched little boy of Constantia's. I shall have to have a word with your father."

"I have not spoken to him for three weeks," said Crispus.

"You ought to get out and about more."

"I did when we first came to Rome. Several of the senators gave parties for me. They were great fun. There's something different about a Roman party. Everything in Nicomedia is so stiff and official. Here things are much more luxurious and at the same time much easier-going. I suppose they've been giving parties longer. I was quite a lion when I first arrived. And the people seemed to have taken a fancy for me. They used to put up a cheer when they saw me. It was all rather jolly. I don't show my face anywhere now."

"What happened?"

"Nothing happened. Nothing ever does happen in the palace. Of course there were a lot of anonymous letters. One gets used to those. It's what *doesn't* happen that gets one down. No one says anything but suddenly you feel you're in disgrace; everyone keeps clear of you. You know you've put your foot in it somewhere but no one says how. I've seen it happen with other fellows. It begins with the eunuchs. They just seem not to notice one. Then the family take it up and then the fellow doesn't appear any more. Someone else moves into his rooms and no one asks anything about him and everything goes on as if he had never existed at all. Sometimes the fellow turns up again. He's just been off somewhere on a job. Usually they never turn up.

"I think Fausta's got something against me. Heaven knows what. We used to be jolly thick together. In fact, I almost thought she was keen on me at one time."

"*Crispus.*"

"Oh, Fausta's always keen on someone. I don't think papa minds. He's far too busy talking religion.

"That's another thing. I can't stand all these clergymen about the place. They're worse than the eunuchs."

"I am a Christian."

"Yes, I know, grandmamma. I'm all for it. I mean it's not my kind of thing, but I'm all for fellows having whatever religion they fancy. But all this arguing night and day about heresy and orthodoxy.

Papa never stops and I don't believe he understands a word of it, any more than I do. And now they talk as if our war in the East had been mixed up in it. It's such rot. My men weren't fighting for Christianity. They were fighting to put papa on top. And we won and he's on top and that's all there is to it. It makes you feel such an ass being told afterwards that you were fighting for religion.

"That's another thing. It isn't for me to say it, but everyone knows I did pretty well in the war. I'm really quite brainy when it comes to fighting. I think I might get some credit for it. I don't care about titles more than the next man but if they are going to make a Caesar, why not me? Why that kid Constantius?

"It's not only clergymen either. The Palatine's full of soothsayers—Sopater and Hermogenes and a frightful old fraud called Nicagoras. Do you know papa sent Nicagoras v.i.p. by Imperial Post to Egypt to attend a magician's congress? I tell you life is hell on the Palatine. I've applied a dozen times to rejoin the army. No reply. Some eunuch just goes off with the papers and that's the last one hears of it."

So Crispus poured out all his grievances long held in silence and Helena's heart yearned towards the baffled hero. At length she said: "I'm sure it's mostly imagination. If there is anything wrong, a word will

put it right. Your father is a *good* man. Remember
that. He's got all sorts of things to worry him and
he may have some bad advisors. But I know my own
son. There's nothing mean about him. I'll go and
see him at once and everything will be all right."

So at length Helena sent a firm message that she
would come to the Palatine and demanded that Constantine fix an hour for her visit.

The guards were at the present, eight deep. Persian carpets were spread on the steps. Trumpets
sounded the royal salute as Helena stepped from her
litter. Constantine was there to embrace her.

It was nearly twenty years since they had met.

Save for his height and his upright carriage, the
conqueror of the world did not seem particularly
military. From the neck down he was all upholstery.
A surcoat of imperial purple, laced with floriations
of gold wire and studded with amorphous pearls,
hung stiff as a carpet to the carpeted floor. It was
sleeveless, and at the arms an undergarment billowed
out, peacock-hued, ending in lace ruffles and a pair
of coarse, much-jewelled hands. Above the surcoat
was a wide collar of gold and enamel, a massive thing
suited to the bull-neck; its miniatures told indifferently the stories of the gospel and of Mount Olym-

pus. Above the collar rose the face, pale now as his father's; he was rouged but purely for ornament; there was no attempt to counterfeit the ruddy complexion of the camp. The surface of the face was in some sort of motion. The Emperor was trying to smile.

But it was none of these things which first caught the notice of Helena.

"My dear boy, what on earth have you got on your head?"

The face above the collar assumed an expression of alarm.

"On my head?" He put up a hand as though to dislodge some bird which might inadvertently have perched there. "Is there anything on my head?"

Two courtiers danced forward. They were shorter than Constantine and made little jumps to see what was amiss. Without excess of ceremony Constantine inclined to them. "Well, what is it? Take it off at once, whatever it is."

The courtiers craned and peered; one raised a finger and touched. They looked at one another. They looked at the Empress Dowager in abject consternation.

"That green wig," said Helena.

Constantine straightened. The courtiers relaxed.

"Oh," he said, "dearest mother. How you frightened me! It's just a little thing I popped on this morning. I have quite a collection. You must ask to see them. Some are *very* pretty. Today I was in such a hurry to see you, I took the first that came to hand. Do you like it?" he asked anxiously. "Do you think it makes me look pale?" He took her hand and led her indoors. "You are not too tired after your journey?"

"I've only come from the Celian."

"I mean your journey from Trèves."

"I have been in Rome three weeks."

"And I was never told! Why was I not told? Until I got your letter yesterday I had no idea you had arrived. I was most anxious about you. Tell me, honestly—no one tells me anything honestly—how do you think I am looking?"

"Pale."

"*Exactly*. I thought as much. They always tell me I look so well and then they overwork me."

Constantine led her through the ante-rooms with slow ceremonious steps. Their way was lined with bowing figures. Helena had expected an intimate conversation in privacy. That, plainly, was not Constantine's plan. She was led to the Throne Room.

Constantine settled himself and waved her to a seat on his right hand only slightly less magnificent than his own. Fausta, who had joined them in their progress, sat on his left. Then the court took its place round and behind them with suitable gradations of obeisance.

"To work, to work," said the Thirteenth Apostle.

"I want to talk to you," said Helena.

"And I to you, dear mother. But duty first. Where are those architects?"

Unlike Diocletian, the fount and origin of all this ceremony, Constantine liked to transact business in full court. For Diocletian pageantry had been a breathing-space, time to think in the intervals of an exacting routine. His real consultations and decisions were made in a study no bigger than a tent, without witnesses so that one precarious life only guarded each secret of state. For Constantine the liturgy of the court was the very substance of royalty. And his secrets were the darker.

"These are the fellows who have been building my arch," he explained, as the chamberlains led forward three men, barefooted, simply dressed, but holding themselves none the less with a certain air among the more splendid throng.

"It is twelve years," said Constantine, "since I

ordered—since the Senate very graciously voted me —a triumphal arch. Why isn't it finished?"

"The Office of Works diverted the labour, sir. Masons are scarce nowadays. They took everyone they could lay hands on for the Christian temples. In spite of that, however, the work *is* to all intents and purposes finished."

"I went there myself yesterday to look at it. It is not finished."

"Certain decorative applications . . ."

"*Certain decorative applications*. You mean the sculptures."

"We meant the sculptures, sir."

"That's precisely what I want to talk about. They are atrocious. A child could do better. Who did them?"

"Titus Carpicius, sir."

"And who is this Titus Carpicius?"

"If you please, sir, I am," said one of the trio.

"My dear," said Fausta. "You must remember Carpicius. I have mentioned him to you often. He is quite the most distinguished sculptor we have."

Constantine seemed not to hear her. He fixed the artist—no stripling; a man of ripe middle age and massive brow—with a frown before which governors and generals trembled. Carpicius glanced at Fausta to assure her that he had taken no offence, and regarded the Emperor with mild patience.

"So you are responsible for those monstrosities I saw yesterday. Perhaps you can explain what they are meant to represent."

"I will try, sir. The arch, as conceived by my friend Professor Emolphus here, is, as you see, on traditional lines, modified to suit modern convention. It is, as you might say, a broad mass broken by apertures. Now this mass involves certain surfaces which Professor Emolphus conceived had about them a certain monotony. The eye was not *held*, if you understand me. Accordingly he suggested that I relieve them with the decorative features you mention. I thought the result rather happy myself. Did you find the shadows too pronounced? They detract from the static quality of the design? I have heard that criticism."

Constantine's patience had been strained by these words. Now he asked icily: "And have you heard this criticism? Your figures are lifeless and expressionless as dummies. Your horses look like children's toys. There is no grace or movement in the whole thing. I've seen better work done by savages. Why, damn it, there's something there that looks like a doll that's supposed to be Me."

"I was not aiming at exact portraiture, sir."

"And why not, pray?"

"It was not the function of the feature."

Constantine turned to his left. "You say this man is the best sculptor in Rome?"

"Everyone says so," said Fausta.

"*Are* you the best sculptor in Rome?"

Carpicius gave a little shrug. There was a silence. Then Professor Emolphus rather bravely intervened. "Perhaps if your Majesty would give us some idea of what exactly you had in mind, the design might be adapted."

"I'll tell you what I had in mind. Do you know the arch of Trajan?"

"Of course."

"What do you think of it?"

"Good of its period," said the Professor, "quite good. Not perhaps the best. I prefer the arch at Benevento on many grounds. But the arch of Trajan is definitely attractive."

"I have the arch of Trajan in mind," said Constantine. "I have never seen the arch at Benevento. I'm not the least interested in the arch at Benevento."

"Your Majesty should really give it your attention. The architrave . . ."

"*I am interested in the arch of Trajan*. I want an arch like that."

"But that was—how long—more than two hundred years ago," said Fausta. "You can't expect one like that today."

"Why not?" said Constantine. "Tell me, why not? The Empire's bigger and more prosperous and more peaceful than it's ever been. I'm always being told so in every public address I hear. But when I ask for a little thing like the arch of Trajan, you say it can't be done. Why not? Could you," he said, turning again on Carpicius, "make me sculpture like that?"

Carpicius looked at him without the least awe. Two forms of pride were here irreconcilably opposed; two prigs stood face to face. "One might, I suppose, contrive some sort of *pastiche*," he said. "It would not be the least significant."

"Damn significance," said Constantine. "Can you do it or can't you?"

"Precisely like that? It is a type of representational work which required a technical virtuosity which you may or may not find attractive—personally I rather do—but the modern artist . . ."

"*Can you do it?*"

"No."

"Well, who can? Find someone else, for God's sake. Professor Emolphus, all I want is a battle with soldiers that look like soldiers and goddesses—I mean traditional symbolic figures —that look like traditional symbolic figures. There must be someone in Rome capable of doing that."

"It is a question of vision as much as virtuosity," said the Professor. "Who can say whether any two people see the same soldier? Who can say how your Majesty sees a soldier?"

"I know what he means, don't you?" said Fausta.

"I see soldiers just as they are on the arch of Trajan. Is there no one in the whole of my empire who can make me soldiers like that?"

"I should very much doubt it."

"Then God damn it, go and pull the carvings off Trajan's arch and stick them on mine. Do it at once. Start this afternoon."

"Spoken like a man, my son," said Helena.

There was more official business of a less humane kind. Constantine liked his audience to hear him at work. Helena grew impatient.

"My son, I came here to see *you*, not the Fiscal Procurator of Moesia."

"In one moment, mamma."

"I want to talk to you about Crispus."

"Yes," said Constantine. "Something must be done about him. But not now. Now we will have prayers. It is a practice I have just instituted. You will approve I am sure."

A little bell was rung and the court arranged itself. Several officials grovelled and left the hall. "The heathen," Constantine explained. The main doors were shut. Deacons emerged from a sacristy with lights, thuribles, a reading-stand and huge books of devotion embossed and enamelled. When everything was ready Constantine, still in his emerald wig, left the throne and was conducted amid clouds of incense to the lectern. First they sang a psalm. Then in a special tone of voice which he had lately grown for the occasion, Constantine fruitily exhorted them: "Oremus." He gave thanks to God for all the blessings of his reign in a detailed autobiography. He mentioned his high birth and eminent suitability for the supreme power, the divine providence which had protected him from the various ills of childhood, his preservation among the daring exploits of his military career. He sketched his irresistible rise to power and the extinction of his many rivals. He gave thanks for his sagacity as a general and as a statesman, providing instances of both. Coming to recent events, he particularized the events of that afternoon not forgetting his mother's presence, the satisfactory report of the Fiscal Procurator of Moesia and the conclusion of the designs for his triumphal arch . . . "per Christum Dominum nostrum." The court sang: "Amen." He then read a passage from one of St. Paul's epistles, briefly expounded its meaning and in silence broken only by the rattle of the thurible, he proceeded with bowed head and clasped hands towards the throne and left the hall by a little door immediately behind it. Fausta slipped out with him.

Helena barely saw them go.

"Where's he off to?" she asked Constantia.

"The private apartments."

"I have a lot to say to him."

"Oh, I don't suppose we shall see him again today. Wasn't the sermon wonderful? He gives us one nearly every day now. Such a treat."

The private apartments had no windows and were massively set in the very centre of the palace. In the lamp-lit study Constantine and Fausta were interviewing two new witches, who had lately been sent from Egypt with a letter of commendation from Nicagoras; an old woman and a girl, both black. The girl was in a trance, stiff as a statue on the table muttering unintelligibly.

Fausta had seen the exhibition before and acted as showman.

"She's completely insensible. You can stick a pin into her. Try."

Constantine stuck. The hysteric continued to mumble showing no signs of discomfort.

"Very amusing," Constantine conceded, sticking again.

"In ordinary life she knows no language except her own. In her trances she speaks Greek, Hebrew and Latin.

"Well, why doesn't she now?" asked the Emperor petulantly. "I can't make out a word she's saying."

"Make her talk," said Fausta to the old woman.

The old woman took the medium by the nose and gently rocked her head from side to side.

"I suppose she wants a present," said Constantine. "They always do."

"She's already been paid."

"Well, send her away if this is all she can do. I can stick pins into people any time I want to. Into people who jump, too. That's much more fun."

Suddenly the young woman sat up and declared very loudly in Latin: "The sacred Emperor is in great danger."

"Yes," said Constantine wearily. "I know. I know. They all say that. Who is it this time?"

"Kiss Crip Cris Kip Crip," babbled the witch and then sank back on the table.

"How do you wake her up?" asked Constantine.

"Kipriscipiscripsip."

"Wake her up," said Fausta.

The old witch bent down and blew hard into the young witch's ear. The eyeballs which had been hidden, emerged; the lids closed; she began to snore. The old witch blew into the other ear. She sat up, stood up, prostrated herself.

"Take her away," said Fausta.

The two Negresses waddled away.

"Not as good as the one we had in Nicomedia," said Constantine.

"But he turned out to be a fraud."

"And this one isn't?"

"What did you think?"

"Well, keep her for a bit. Go and see her sometimes. Report if she has anything really interesting."

"I believe she must have been trying to say Crispus."

"Well, why didn't she? No one ever seems to talk sense to me nowadays."

Fausta went to her bath, which was the most luxurious in the world, with a sense of discouragement. As she lay in the balmy steam she tried to fix her mind on "Homoousion" and "Homoiousion." Often those magical words had the power to soothe her. But not that day.

"Oh, very well then. Licinianus too," said Constantine and sighed. "Anyone else?"

"Constantia," said Fausta, cool as fish. "Constantine, Dalmatius Annibabianus, Dalmatius Caesar, Dalmatius Rex, Constantius Flavius, Basilina, Anastasia, Bassianus, Eutropia, Nepotianus, Flavius Popilius Nepotianus."

"Were they all in it? Why, Flavius Popilius Nepotianus was only christened yesterday. I chose the names for him."

"Better send them all to Pola together. It will save trouble in the long run."

"Trouble," said Constantine crossly. "I've had nothing but trouble since I came to Rome. You drive me too hard. Besides I have to prepare my sermon on Regeneration. Everyone is looking forward to it so much. I've done quite enough for one day. Crispus and Licinianus can go. The rest must wait."

He scrawled his name to the order, popped on a wig and shuffled away to his private oratory.

It was briefly stated in the Court Circular that Crispus and Licinianus had gone abroad on a special mission. Everyone know what that meant. On the Palatine no one mentioned the affair. In the freer world outside a few patricians wondered over their wine: "Why Licinianus? Who next?"

In the streets a couplet was circulated:

Who wants the olden golden age of heroes?
For us the diamond and ruby—Nero's.

But there was little curiosity. For a long time now the Romans had grown accustomed to the succession of grim, adroit families who emerged from the Balkans and destroyed themselves. The Jubilee, thank heavens, was nearly over. Soon the court would pack and leave The City to its proper concerns.

On the Palatine the unspoken question "Who next?" was in every heart; a more lively question than "Why Licinianus?"; but the days passed and as the courtiers looked anxiously about them they found everyone still in his usual place. It seemed that this was purely a family affair.

Constantine did not appear. He was known to be

in one of his moods. There were no more sermons. Fausta alone had the entrée. The highest officials had to work through her. They gave her papers and from time to time she gave them back, signed. She alone knew the Emperor's condition.

They had been through many of these moods of his, he and she together. This was something blacker and deeper than ever before. It had come on him quite suddenly. He was at his most bland, his sermons were at their most elevated pitch, for the first few days after Crispus's departure. Then without warning he cancelled all audiences and took to his room. There he lay, hour after hour, in his shift, in the feeble lamplight, wigless, unpainted, tearful, in an intermittent stupor of melancholy. Fausta stayed by him. It was no time to let his fancies run free.

Three days after his change, when the prison ship was already at Pola, he ordered its recall. He said he wished to speak to Crispus. He asked for him repeatedly until Fausta found herself obliged preposterously to break the news to him of his son's death. What had he died of? Fausta improvised a story of plague on the Dalmatian coast. Crispus had insisted on going ashore, had died in twelve hours, was cremated there at once for fear of infection.

Constantine fell into a paroxysm of grief and then

demanded more details. What were the symptoms? What remedies had been attempted? What were the names and qualifications of the attendant doctors? Was there no suspicion of foul play?

She remarked that Crispus had not suffered alone. His little cousin Licinianus had succumbed too, with several of their closest entourage. It had been a very virulent kind of plague.

This seemed to comfort Constantine for a time. He lay still muttering: "Swelling in the groin . . . black vomit . . . coma . . . putrefaction" until hours later he said: "That is not at all how I intended them to die: I gave quite different, quite explicit orders for their murder."

"It was not murder. They were executed for treason. It was necessary."

"It was not necessary at all," said Constantine severely. "I would sooner, far sooner, it had never happened."

"It was your life or his."

"Well, what's the difference?"

It was not an easy question to answer. Constantine repeated: "Tell me the difference. Why is it 'necessary' that *I* should live rather than anyone else?"

"You are the Emperor."

"So was your father. That didn't keep him alive. I killed him. He was a beast, anyway."

The beastliness of the Emperor Maximian proved a consoling topic. Constantine expatiated, Fausta mildly assented. Then he fell into another long silence, all that night, all next day, and when he spoke it was to renew the former topic. "Everyone is always telling me that it is so necessary for me to live. It must be, I suppose. There seems to be unanimous agreement on the subject. But I can't see any reason in it."

So the days of the black mood wore on, until at length he said: "Is my mother still in Rome?"

"I believe so."

"Why hasn't she come to see me? She must have heard how unwell I am. Do you think she can be angry with me about anything?"

This was the question above all others which Fausta wished to avoid. The Empress Dowager was very angry indeed and she had come to the Palatine daily since the announcement of Crispus's death, demanding her son. They told her he had been called away to quell a mutiny; that he had left suddenly for Benevento to get ideas for the completion of his arch. Helena had not believed a word of it. True daughter of the house of Boadicea she had stormed about the palace from room to room driving before her a scurry of eunuchs and prelates. Only the impenetrable intricacy of the ground-plan baffled her till now. One day she would find the entrance to Constantine's apartments and, when she did, no sentry would withstand her.

"She was very fond of Crispus," Fausta ventured to say.

"Yes, naturally. She brought him up, you know. He was a dear little boy."

It was then that Fausta conceived her one egregious mistake.

"I can't help wondering," she said, "whether perhaps your mother didn't know something about the plot."

The very tone resounded in Constantine's disordered mind. It was familiar and peculiar. How many had Fausta not undone in just those accents? Constantine listened intently and heard the death knell of old comrades-in-arms—villains mostly—hacked, strangled, poisoned one after another, in the ups and downs of twenty years of married life. He said nothing. She continued: "Crispus visited her at the Sessorian Palace, we know. It was just at the time when she arrived in Rome that the plot came to a head."

Constantine said nothing. Fausta was accustomed to these pauses. Presently to keep the subject alive, she asked: "Where did your mother come from originally? No one seems to know."

"Britain. It was one of my father's few secrets." And as though he had forgotten the subject of their conversation he began to talk about that remote island, of the white walls of York and the rich poetic legends of the place, saying he hoped one day to revisit it.

It seemed to Fausta that her first attempt had failed. It was like being a sower, she thought, like the sower in the Gospel. Sometimes seed fell on stony ground. She could try again. Thus she reasoned that afternoon while Constantine lay silently regarding her, but after her bath, refreshed and restored to good humour, meeting the same hard stare, she felt glad that her hint had passed unrecognized. The old lady could not be a serious danger. She would soon go back to Trèves and not be seen again. Never do harm except for positive, immediate advantage. Beyond that simple rule, Fausta held, lay disaster and perhaps damnation.

Fausta came from her bath oily and aromatic and Constantine seemed more aware of her presence than hitherto. She wondered whether perhaps he was amorous. Sometimes his black moods ended in that way. She invited; he ignored; stony ground again. It was not that. Constantine had something to think about. He thought *Fausta had gone too far.*

That evening Constantine called for the witches. Fausta, in the mood of calculation which her bath induced, had decided that their usefulness was over. This should be their last performance. It was.

The girl was thrown into her trance with a few passes. She writhed and grunted and muttered as she had done before at many a fateful séance. Constantine watched. Presently she said, as she usually did: "The sacred Emperor is in great danger." It was all going according to routine. She sat quite rigid, her breathing almost ceased; her teeth were set, her eyeballs turned up, as they had seen her time and again. Then a change came over her. She broke into a sweat, relaxed, smiled, rolled her eyes easily and began gently and rhythmically swaying and thumping. The old witch looked worried and whispered to Fausta.

"Something has gone wrong. The old woman says that she had better wake her. There will be no prophecy tonight."

Music, unheard by the three watchers, was sounding in the girl's heart, drumming from beyond the pyramids, wailing in the *bistro* where the jazz disc spun. She had stepped off the causeway of time and place into trackless swamp. She was anybody's baby now, caught as it were out of her shell, quite defence-less. And thus wandering and groping the hysteric was suddenly seized by a demon and possessed. From her full young lips broke the ancient tortured voice of prophecy; in soft tones, rhythmical as the beat of the tom-toms, sweet and low like a love song.

Zivio! Viva! Arriba! Heil!
Plenty big chief from the Rhine to the Nile.
He got two gods and he got two wives,
Got a heap of chips worth a million lives.

Shook the bones for the world and The City,
Threw himself a natural and scooped the kitty.
Gobbles his chop in tip-top style,
Plenty big chief for Helena's isle.

Man of destiny, man of grief
Nobody loved that plenty big chief.
The world was his baby, but baby got sore.
So he lost the world and plenty lives more.
Threw him snake's eyes, lost all the pile,
Lost to the world on Helena's isle.

Gazing on the ocean, all alone,
Saddest chief that ever was known,
Nothing but the ocean for mile on mile.

Played for a sucker by British guile,
Tied up tight in durance vile
And left there to rot on Helena's isle.
Ave atque vale! Heil!

She ceased and the old witch looked abjectly at her patrons. She blew in the girl's ears and shook her and issued sharp commands in her own language.

"I think we have heard enough," said Constantine. "Let us go." And for the first time for weeks he left the private apartments.

"That was quite the most remarkable performance she has given," said Fausta.

"Most remarkable."

"Did you notice how she mentioned 'British' guile?"

"I did."

"No one knows, do they, about your mother?"

"No one except you and me, my dear."

"Well, I call that proof positive the girl is genuine."

"Proof positive," said Constantine.

He went to the great hall where he conducted his business. He called for a wig. He called for papers. The court assembled about him. With great despatch he finished off a number of outstanding cases. Word went round everywhere that the Emperor's mood was over.

The Lord Chamberlain brought him a list of those who had applied for audiences.

"The Empress Dowager every day?"

"Every day."

"I will see her tomorrow. And I shall make an inspection of the arch. Have the architects there to meet me. No prayers today."

He withdrew with an officer whom he employed from time to time on confidential business.

"Those two witches," he said. "The black ones Nicagoras sent me. I shan't want them any more."

"Very good, sir."

"You've been keeping them shut up?"

"Oh, yes, sir. Ever since they arrived."

"Well, have them destroyed."

"Very good, sir."

"They've seen no one?"

"Only the Empress."

"Ah, yes, the Empress. I want to talk about her, too. Where is she exactly at the moment?"

"I suppose in her bath. It is the usual time."

At the usual time, the good time, there in the torrid room, quite alone and quite naked Fausta gazed into the unclouded mirror—for the heat was dry as

the desert—and studied her round, moist, serene
face, and meditated.

Twenty years married, surrounded by spies, and
not once caught in a peccadillo; the mother of six
and still—surely?—deeply desirable; not yet forty,
and mistress of the world.

Quite lately the upholsterers had completed the
comfort of this little room with a mattress and cushions of delicate African goatskin; a triumph of the
tanner, soft as silk, impermeable, with all the tang
of leather artfully drowned in an oil of sandalwood.

This, the hot dry room was of its nature the plain-
est. Objects of art stood in the piscina and the esedra.
Here even the door had to be simple. Bronze grew
too hot and the marquetry of ivory and tortoise-shell
which was part of the first design, fell to pieces. This
door was a mere slab of polished cedar. But the walls
and floor and ceiling were from drawings by Emolphus, elaborate and dazzling as a Persian rug. The
lapidaries of the world had contributed their showi-
est colours and oddest veins for its construction.

Fausta watched the sweat trickle between her
breasts and overbrim her navel. She was content.
To out-live one's enemies in this world; to have the
dear Bishop always at hand to commit one, when it
became necessary, to immediate, eternal felicity in

the next; what heroine of antiquity enjoyed Fausta's privileges?

But surely the boiler-men were rather overdoing it this evening?

She reviewed the unforeseen drama of that evening's séance. There really was no natural, rational explanation. Unprompted, unrehearsed, inspired one might almost say, the little Negress had stepped out where Fausta hesitated and had said the one thing that was so precisely needed. And Fausta had been on the point of having the girl strangled. It simply showed the paramount importance of the supernatural. It was all true, what the Bishop described, the whole flighty beneficent world of Cherubim and Seraphim and guardian angels. Heaven had spoken to her as it spoke to Constantine at the Milvian Bridge.

But it was definitely getting too hot. Fausta rang the bell.

Waiting for the slave who ought instantly to have been at her side and was now unaccountably tardy, Fausta meditated on this joyful mystery. Why was she, alone among women, so uniquely privileged? It could scarcely be a tribute to her great position in the world. In fact, when one came to think of it, Divine Providence seemed ostentatiously neglectful of the imperial family. No, it was something in herself; some rare idiosyncrasy of soul. Unworthily, perhaps, but most conveniently, she was the elect of God; His own especial favourite and consort. Eusebius, more than once, had hinted at something of the kind. Now there was plain proof.

But no one came to the bell. It was really getting unpleasantly, intolerably hot. When she sat up her movement seemed to fan the scorching air about her and her heart began to thump unhealthily. She put her foot to the blistering floor and hastily withdrew it. She rang the bell furiously, fearfully. Something was wrong. No one came and the blood drummed in her ears the witch's rhythm *The world was her baby, but baby got sore.*

It was only three paces across the pavement of malachite and porphyry. They had to be taken. Careful to the last she made stepping stones of the cushions and so reached the door; resolutely took hold of the searing handle, turned and pushed but it did not move. She had known it would not. Somewhere, between one cushion and the next, she had come to herself; had seen through the panel the bolts beyond. No use now to push or ring or knock. The good hour was over. She slid and floundered and presently lay still, like a fish on a slab.

CHAPTER NINE

Recessional

"I KNOW, I *know*. Everything you say, my dear mother, is perfectly true. It just isn't kind, that's all, and at a time like this one looks for a little kindness especially from a mother.

"I haven't been at all myself lately. I get these moods from time to time. Don't please imagine for an instant that I enjoy them. They're an absolute torment to me. I've seen doctors about it—the very best opinions in the world. They can't help. It's just the price one has to pay for superior abilities. That's what they all tell me.

"Well, other people have got to pay the price too. They can't expect to have everything done for them for nothing. Here am I working myself to death for them, clearing away all their enemies, managing the whole world for them. And if at times I get a bit moody they talk about me as though I were a monster.

"Oh, yes, I know what they are saying, all over Rome. I hate Rome. I think it's a perfectly beastly place. It never has agreed with me. Even after my battle at the Milvian Bridge when everything was flags and flowers and hallelujahs and I was the Saviour— even then I didn't feel quite at ease. Give me the East where a man can feel unique. Here you are just one figure in an endless historical pageant. The City is waiting for you to move on.

"What's more, immorality is rife. I couldn't repeat the things I've heard. It's all falling down too, and the drains are shocking. I tell you I *hate* the place."

"You spoke of it once as the Holy City."

"That, my dear mother, was before my Enlightenment. Before I saw the great dawn in the East. I hate Rome. I'd like to burn it down."

"Like Nero?"

"Now why did you say that? You've seen that beastly rhyme. Someone left it yesterday among my papers. *'For us the diamond and ruby—Nero's.'* That's just the kind of thing the Romans are saying about me. How dare they? How can they be so *stupid?* In Nicomedia they call me the Thirteenth Apostle.

"It's all the fault of that woman. Things will be better now she's gone, quite different. It was all Fausta's fault. You couldn't believe the things I've learned about her during the past twenty-four hours.

Everything was Fausta's fault. We'll start again. We'll have an entirely new deal."

"My son, there is only one way in which things can be made new."

"I know what you mean," said Constantine. He looked calculating; suddenly the politician. "Everyone is always hinting at it. *Baptism*. Fausta used positively to nag me about baptism; even Constantia.

"Damn it," he added in a burst of indignation. "Constantia is all right, isn't she? I've done nothing to *her*, have I? And yet they compare me to Nero. Would *he* have left her safe and smiling?"

"Not smiling, Constantine."

"Well, she ought to be. She had a very narrow squeak, I can tell you. But that's typical. No gratitude anywhere. Why isn't Constantia smiling?" Helena said nothing and Constantine repeated furiously: *"Why isn't Constantia smiling? I'll have her here and make her smile. I'll . . .* Mother, am I mad?"

Helena still said nothing. After a pause Constantine said: "Let me tell you about my Moods, as they call them. Let me explain why it is so fatuously unfair to compare me to Nero. Let me explain exactly, once and for all, about my Moods. I want you to understand.

"Nero had moods. I've read about them. He was a beastly person—a neurotic aesthete. He positively enjoyed destroying things and seeing people suffer. I'm just the opposite. All I live for is other people—teaching them, keeping them out of mischief, putting up buildings for them. Look what I've done even here in Rome. Look at the churches and the endowments. Do I have favourites? I haven't even a friend. Do I give orgies? Do I dance and sing and get tipsy? Do I ever enjoy myself at all in any way? I should think my receptions are about the dullest parties ever given on the Palatine. I just work. Sometimes I feel as though the whole world had come to a standstill except for myself; as though everyone were just gaping, for *me* to do something for them. They're scarcely human beings; just *things,* in the way, in the wrong place, that have to be moved and put to use or thrown away. Nero thought he was God. A most blasphemous and improper idea. I know I am human. In fact I often feel that I am the only real human being in the whole of creation. And that's not pleasant at all, I can assure you. Do you understand at all, mother?"

"Oh, yes, perfectly."

"What is it, then?"

"Power without Grace," said Helena.

"Now you are going to start nagging about baptism again."

"Sometimes," Helena continued, "I have a terrible dream of the future. Not now, but presently, people may forget their loyalty to their kings and emperors and take power for themselves. Instead of letting one victim bear this frightful curse they will take it all on themselves, each one of them. Think of the misery of a whole world possessed of Power without Grace."

"Yes, yes. That's all very well, but why should *I* be the victim?"

"We talked of it years ago—do you remember?—when you were on your way to Britain to your father. I have always remembered your words. You said: 'If I wish to live, I must determine to rule' "

"And that is true today."

"But not without Grace, Constantine."

"*Baptism*. It always comes back to that in the end. Well, I'm going to be baptized, never fear. But not yet. In my own time. I've got other things to do before that. You do truly believe, don't you, in all the priests say?"

"Of course."

"So do I. And *that's* the whole point. There are some lunatics in Africa who say that once you are converted, properly, you can never sin again. I know that's not true. You've only got to look round you to see that it's not. Look at Fausta. But baptism, just for the moment, washes away all the sins of your life, doesn't it? That's what they say. That's what we believe, isn't it?"

"Yes."

"You start again, quite new, quite innocent, like a newborn child. But next minute you can fall into sin again and be damned to all eternity. That's good doctrine, isn't it? Well, then, what does the wise man do—the man in a position like mine where it's impossible not to commit a few sins every now and then? He waits. He puts it off till the very last moment. He lets the sins pile up blacker and heavier. It doesn't matter. They'll be washed away in baptism, the whole lot of them, and then all he has to do is to stay innocent, just for a very short time, just to hold the devil at bay for a week or two, perhaps a few hours only. It shouldn't be too difficult. That's strategy, you see. I've got it all planned.

"Of course there's a hazard. One might be caught unawares, ambushed before one had time for the final *coup*. That's why I have to be so particularly careful. I can't afford to take any chances. That's what the secret police are for, and the fortune-tellers.

Most of what they tell me is nonsense, I know, but one can never be sure. There might be something in it. One must act according to one's information. That's tactics. You see it's not just my life that's at stake; it's my immortal soul. And that's infinitely important, isn't it? Literally, *infinitely* important. The priests admit it. So you see it doesn't really matter so very much if Crispus was innocent or not. What are a few years less or more in Licinianus's life? We're dealing with quite another scale of values.

"Have I explained myself? Do you see now how cruelly unfair it is to compare me with Nero? . . . All I need is to be understood and appreciated. I know what I'll do," he continued, brightening. "If you promise not to be angry with me any more I'll show you Something Very Special."

He led her to the sacristy that opened from the great hall of the palace. He called for keys and with his own hands opened a cupboard; inside stood a tall parcel, swathed in silk. A sacristan offered assistance. "Go away," Constantine said. "No one is allowed to touch this except myself. Very few have even seen it."

With eager clumsiness he unwrapped his exhibit and then stood clear, posing grandly with it in his right hand.

The thing was the size and shape of a military standard. Its head formed a Latin cross, gold-plated. Above was a jewelled wreath of elaborate design and in the centre of the wreath a jewelled monogram, the sacred XP. From the crossbar hung a banner of purple satin richly embroidered and gemmed, bearing the motto ΤΟΥΤΩ ΝΙΚΑ and a series of delicately stitched medallion portraits.

"What on earth have you got there?" asked Helena.

"Can't you *see*. It's *It*, my Labarum."

Helena studied this magnificent piece of arts-and-crafts with growing bewilderment. "You don't mean to say that you carried *that* into action at the Milvian Bridge."

"Of course. In this sign I conquered."

"But, Constantine, the story as I always heard it was that you had a vision on the eve of the battle and that then and there you changed the markings on the troops' shields and had the armourer knock you up your own standard in the shape of the cross."

"Certainly. This is it."

"And you had this made in camp?"

"Yes. Isn't it interesting?"

"But it must have taken months to make."

"Two or three hours, I assure you. The jewellers were inspired. Everything was miraculous that day."

"And whose are the portraits?"

"My own and my children's."

"But, my dear boy, they weren't all born then."

"I tell you it was a miracle," said Constantine huffily. "If you're not interested I'll put it away."

"Take the place," said Constantine to Pope Sylvester. "It's all yours. I am leaving and I shan't come back—ever. You can pack whoever you like into my sarcophagus. I shall leave my bones in the East when I die . . . if I do die. You know, one can never be sure; I've been thinking a lot about it lately and reading it up; there are quite a number of authenticated cases—are there not?—when God for His own good reasons has dispensed with all that degrading business of getting ill and dying and decaying. Sometimes I feel that in His bountiful mercy He may have something of the kind in store for me. I can't quite imagine myself dying in the ordinary way. Perhaps He will send a chariot, as He did for the prophet Elias . . . It wouldn't really surprise me at all— nor anyone else, I daresay."

Helena here caught Sylvester's eye. They understood one another.

The Emperor's musing ceased and he continued, more practically. "But not, in any case, for many years. There is so much to be done. When the time comes my sarcophagus empty or—er—occupied must lie in Christian surroundings. Rome is heathen and always will be. Yes, I know, you've got the tombs of Peter and Paul. I hope I have not shown myself insensible to that distinction. But why are they here? Simply because the Romans murdered them. That's the plain truth. Why, they even thought of murdering *me*. It's an ungodly place, your holiness, and you're welcome to it.

"One must start something *new*. I've got the site, very central; it will make a sublime port. The plans are drawn. Work will start at once on a great *Christian* capital, in the very centre of Christendom; a city built round two great new churches dedicated to—what do you think?—Wisdom and Peace. The idea came quite suddenly the other day, as my best ideas do come to me. Some might call it 'inspiration.' To me it merely seems natural. You can have your old Rome, Holy Father, with its Peter and Paul and its tunnels full of martyrs. *We* start with no unpleasant associations; in innocence, with Divine Wisdom and Peace. I shall set up my Labarum there," he added, with a severe look at his mother, "where it will be appreciated. As for the old Rome, it's yours."

"To quote the judicious Gaius, 'a ruinous legacy,' " remarked one domestic prelate to another.

"But I rather wish we had it in writing all the same."

"We will, monsignore. We will."

"Unpleasant associations are the seed of the Church," said Pope Sylvester.

"Lactantius used to say something like that."

"Oh, there's nothing new about it. I never try to be original. That sort of thing's better left to the Levantines."

"I don't like new things," said Helena. "No one does in the land I come from. I don't like Constantine's idea of a New Rome. It sounds so empty and clean, like the newly swept house in the gospel that was filled with devils."

They were getting along together famously, these two admirable old people. Helena had stayed behind after Constantine's departure, and the Pope had seemed to expect it.

"You can't just send for Peace and Wisdom, can you?" Helena continued, "and build houses for them and shut them in. Why, they don't exist at all except *in people,* do they? Give me real bones every time."

They were in a small loggia overlooking what had once been the park, now almost filled by Constantine's new church.

"It's odd to think that poor Fausta once lived here."

In Fausta's day these neat clerical offices had been festooned with silk. Nothing of it survived. Here and there in the palace the Laterans might be remembered by a section of cornice or by an ivy-grown satyr in the park. But there was nothing of Fausta's. She had passed with a winking gold fin and a line of bubbles. Even the two Eusebiuses had struck her name from their prayers.

Helena followed the thread of unhappy recent memories and said: "Not that Rome has been all I expected."

"I hear that so often. I can't judge. I am pure Roman myself. I can't imagine what it would be like to come here for the first time."

"I knew a man once—he was my tutor at home—who used to tell me about the holy cities of Asia. They are so holy, he said, that their walls shut out all the evil passions of the world. You have only to set foot there to become like the saints."

"Had he been to those places?"

"Oh, no, he was just a slave."

"I don't suppose he would have found them so

very different from anywhere else. Slaves like to
imagine such cities. I daresay they always will. To a
Roman there can only be one City, and that a very
imperfect place indeed."

"It is imperfect, isn't it?"

"Yes, of course."

"Getting worse?"

"No, I think a little better. We look back already
to the time of the persecution as though it were the
heroic age, but have you ever thought how awfully
few martyrs there were, compared with how many
there ought to have been? The Church isn't a cult
for a few heroes. It is the whole of fallen mankind
redeemed. And of course just at the moment we're
getting a lot of rather shady characters rolling in, just
to be on the winning side."

"What do they believe, these shady characters?
What goes on in their minds?"

"God alone knows."

"It's the one question I've been asking all my life,"
said Helena. "I can't get a straight answer even here
in Rome."

"There are people in this city," said Sylvester quite
cheerfully, "who believe that the Emperor was preparing a bath of children's blood to cure himself of
the measles. I cured him instead and that is why

he has been so generous to me. People believe that here and now while the Emperor and I are alive and going about in front of their faces. What will they believe in a thousand years' time?"

"And some of them don't seem to believe anything at all," said Helena. "It's all a game of words."

"I know," said Sylvester, "I know."

And then Helena said something which seemed to have no relevance. "Where *is* the cross, anyway?" she asked.

"What cross, my dear?"

"The only one. The real one."

"I don't know. I don't think anyone knows. I don't think anyone has ever asked before."

"It must be somewhere. Wood doesn't just melt like snow. It's not three hundred years old. The temples here are full of beams and panelling twice that age. It stands to reason God would take more care of the cross than of them."

"Nothing 'stands to reason' with God. If He had wanted us to have it, no doubt He would have given it to us. But he hasn't chosen to. He gives us enough."

"But how do you know He *doesn't* want us to have it—the cross, I mean? I bet He's just waiting for one of us to go and find it—just at this moment when it's most needed. Just at this moment when everyone is forgetting it and chattering about the hypostatic union, there's a solid chunk of wood waiting for them to have their silly heads knocked against. I'm going off to find it," said Helena.

The Empress Dowager was an old woman, almost of an age with Pope Sylvester, but he regarded her fondly as though she were a child, an impetuous young princess who went well to hounds, and he said with the gentlest irony: "You'll tell me, won't you?—if you are successful."

"I'll tell the world," said Helena.

CHAPTER TEN

The Innocence of
Bishop Macarius

HELENA started on her pilgrimage in the early autumn of the year 326. Nicomedia was the starting-point. There, at that time, the communications of the Empire converged. There the limitless resources of the Treasury were put at her disposal. The official machine smoothly prepared her way and equipped her caravan.

She moved at an easy pace, going out of her way and pausing at Drepanum to order a church for St. Lucian, then turning inland to the trunk road through Ancyra, Tarsus, Antioch and Lydda. Wherever she went with her mixed task-force of guards and her train of bullion, she was greeted by clergy and officials and populace, prostrating themselves and applauding. She endowed convents, freed prisoners, dowered orphans, directed the building of shrines and basilicas. She saw the sights and she venerated the scenes of Christian history. She gave huge tips to the hierarchy. She moved in a golden haze of benefaction, welcomed, it seemed, and dearly be-

197

loved of all. She could not know the dismay which her approach was causing in one innocent breast.

For Macarius, Bishop of Aelia Capitolina, was most certainly innocent. He well knew that false accusations were as distasteful to God as evasions and concealments. He had been into the whole matter, again and again, minutely, and found no breath of impure motive anywhere in his whole conduct.

When Macarius examined his conscience it was with the method and trained observation of a field-naturalist in a later age studying the life of a pond. Less scientific penitents noted merely the few big fish; the squeamish recoiled from the weed and scum and with closed eyes blurted out an emotional, inaccurate tale of self-reproach. But through all his long life the Bishop had refined his knowledge of the soul until each opacity, each microscopic germ had a peculiar significance for him. He knew what was noxious, what was harmless, what was of value. So, now, in the great matter of the Holy Sepulchre he gazed through fathoms of limpid sweet water and pronounced himself blameless.

And yet he *was* being blamed, by the Prefect among others. It was the Prefect who first brought the news, coming to call on the Bishop one warm September morning and spoiling a day of promised calm.

"You see what you've done now," said the Prefect. "I hope you're satisfied."

The very fact of the Prefect coming to call showed how things had changed for Macarius in the last eighteen months. Two years ago the Prefect would have sent for him to Government House. A few years before that he would either have denied all knowledge of Macarius's existence or clapped him in gaol.

"How in God's name," asked the Prefect, "do you think I can put up the Empress Dowager? It was a miserable enough place even before you started messing about with it. Now what with builders and pilgrims and half the streets up, it simply isn't habitable. How am I going to protect her? The only thing they haven't increased is *my* establishment."

"Believe me," said Bishop Macarius, "I really am very sorry about it. I never intended anything like this to happen."

It had begun at Nicaea the Summer before. That opportunity was unique. For the first time in history the Church appeared in her majesty—the Papal legates, the Emperor, the assembled hierarchy of all Christendom. Many of the higher clergy had complaints against one another of heresy, treachery and magic. Constantine burned these, ostensibly unread.

But Macarius had a petition of another order. Small-minded men might impute self-seeking to him, but Macarius knew better. He willed nothing except the greater glory of God and this high purpose was being frustrated by a vexatious anomaly in the position of his own see.

For his Aelia Capitolina was nothing less than the ancient, holy city of Jerusalem, the very umbilical point of Christian devotion. In and about this little garrison town God's chosen people had fulfilled their destiny. Here Our Lord and His Blessed Mother were born, had died and ascended to heaven. Here the Holy Ghost had fallen in tongues of fire upon the newborn Church. Macarius was hourly appalled by his own unworthiness to set up his throne on the scene of these events. He would gladly have made way for a more powerful man if by that means he could secure for the holy city the honour due to it. But in fact it was scarcely honoured at all. A quirk of the civil administration made it a suffragan see and, what was the more bitter, suffragan to Caesarea, a place of little history and that little, bad; the creation of Herod, a commercial port reeking of idolatry, officialdom and vice. That anomaly must be righted sooner or later. But Macarius might have shrunk from pressing his own claims and left the matter to time, had there not been a reason for extreme urgency. Eusebius of Caesarea was not a man he could serve with a good conscience. He was a politician and man-of-letters, a supercilious, unscrupulous man, a fit ally for his namesake of Nicomedia and, like him, deep in the black heart of the Arian conspiracy. There were maimed veterans of the persecution in Caesarea who, when they saw their Bishop going about his high affairs, remarked that they had seen him passing in and out of the prison compound in just that way, elegant, self-possessed, bearing neat little rolls of manuscript, when they lay in chains; an apostate, perhaps an informer.

Macarius could not expose his clergy and his people to that malign influence. But he stated his claim at Nicaea on the first consideration alone.

The Council was sympathetic and passed a noncommittal resolution. He was given the pallium and a private audience. The Emperor was positively affable. Macarius reminded him of the glories of Zion. The Emperor seemed captivated. Was it then perhaps that his shadowy mind saw in a first reflected gleam the opposed faces of history and myth? The new religion with which he busied himself had many attractions; it inculcated a convenient ethic of brotherhood, peace and obedience; it offered powerful magical rewards of protection, forgiveness and immortality. But had Constantine ever made a distinction between the stories that were told of Galilee and those of Olympus? Now for the first time he was talking face to face with a man who handled, who held in his particular charge, the identical wreath of thorn which had crowned the dying God three hundred years ago.

"Can you be sure?"

"But, of course, sir. Ever since that day the Church of Jerusalem has guarded it. Mary herself picked it up and carried it home. It went with them to Pella and returned with them when the laws were relaxed. We have the spear, too, you know, which pierced His side, and many other things of the kind."

"Extraordinary," said the Emperor, adding the eternal querulous protest of baffled authority. "Why was I never told?"

Macarius told him: all about Jerusalem; of how through all its vicissitudes the Christian haunted it, ruined or rebuilt, and so kept continuous and alive the secret tradition of the holy places; of the Garden of Gethsemane, the upper room of the Last Supper, the sorrowful way from court-house to Calvary.

Thus quite naturally, inevitably, he was led on

to speak of the project nearest his heart. He had come to Nicaea hoping to interest somebody in it, never hoping for this golden propitious moment of confidence.

"And then," he said, "there is, of course, the holiest of all the holy places—the sepulchre itself."

"You know where that is?"

"Within a few yards. The Emperor Hadrian buried it two hundred years ago when he laid out the new city. People say he did so deliberately to suppress the cult and built the temple of Venus on it as an insult. But I doubt very much whether he knew of its existence. The Christians used to go there in ones and twos after dark. It was all kept very quiet for fear the authorities would destroy it. What they did in effect was to preserve it. I expect that the engineers just drew their plans from the map without considering the matter at all. It was providential that they covered it up. They might so easily have cut it clean away. It wouldn't be at all a big task to uncover it again."

Not at all a big task! How often Macarius had looked at that broad, crowded terrace, sick at heart for what was below. The trees in the little garden were gnarled, the paving had been worn and renewed and worn again, the statue, even, had mellowed in two centuries and lost something of its impudicity. The whole place proclaimed its permanence. O for the Faith that moved mountains! This was something quite beyond the hope of human accomplishment. Not till the end of the world, perhaps, would that treasure come to light.

So Macarius had thought during the days of persecution. But now the trumpets everywhere were sounding for victory, and here was he talking with the Emperor, the source of all material power. The thing was quite easy. Just the shovelling up of a heap of dust. And thus Constantine saw it. He gave the order like a housewife having a cupboard cleared.

"Certainly," he said. "Start at once, as soon as you get back. I'll see you get all the labour you need. Do the thing properly. Make a decent job of it."

Was it a decent job? That was the question which drove Macarius back and back again into his own innocent conscience, to learn how things had gone wrong. It was a year, now, since the interview at Nicaea. Wonders had indeed been performed but Macarius was not happy.

The first excavations were easy enough. The site which the Christians had always pointed out as the scene of the Crucifixion and Resurrection lay almost in the centre of the new town. There was no trace now above ground of the walls which had once run near it. Aelia Capitolina lay flat across them, half out of what had once been the old city; a rectangle set down by the planners among hills and valleys and ruins and dry waterworks. It might have lain in Britain or Africa; a standard, second-century garrison-town. The temple of Venus, the garden and the cross-roads stood on what had once been a little gulley between rocky hills. Hadrian's engineers had filled it with rubble—there was no lack of that—and levelled it. Constantine's engineers now swept it clear. There was no difficulty in distinguishing the natural rock when they struck it. In a few months the whole site lay exposed, the two little hills plainly evident and the dip between them. The smaller hill was Golgotha. Thirty yards distant, half-way up the opposing slope was a tomb, a step down, a perpendicular rock face cut in the hillside, a low door, a vestibule and the inner chamber where the sacred body had lain; all just as Macarius had pictured it.

Countless times in his meditations Macarius had trodden the road to Golgotha pausing at each sad station. He had stood benighted beside the three crosses and lingered, when the rest had gone home, at the blocked tomb with Mary Magdalen and Mary

the Mother of God. It was home ground, this acre
of rock, a patrimony reclaimed. He was quite at his
ease rejoicing on his knees in the little cave.

News of the operation flashed to Constantine from
tower to tower of the chain of signal-posts that ran
from Caesarea to Nicomedia. It came at the right
moment. Constantine had newly arrived cross and
dispirited and lonely from his Roman holiday. He
needed something of just this kind, some new resounding conquest, another miracle. And here it
was, a sure pledge that anything untoward which
had happened on the Palatine was forgiven and forgotten and that he was back again in the full un-
shaded glare of Divine favour.

He wrote at once, exuberantly, to Macarius:

*How God loves Us! Words fail. Victorious in war,
free in conscience. We are now the recipients of a
stupendous revelation, hidden for generations—the
sepulchre itself, the original monument of the Passion
and Resurrection. The mind boggles. This just shows
how right We were to accept the Christian religion. See
that they don't put back that idolatrous temple. We will
build a church there instead; the finest church in the
world, better than every other in every detail. You and
the Governor and Dracilianus must see to this. Just
ask for whatever you need. How many columns will it
take? How much other marble? Make it strong and*

gorgeous. Write and tell me what to send. This is a unique place and needs unique treatment. Would you prefer the roof domed or flat? If the former, it should be gilded. Get your estimates out as soon as you can. How about the rafters and wood panelling, if you decide on a flat roof? Let me know. God bless you, dear Brother.

That was the letter, brimming with benevolence, which shook the Bishop from his mood of placid rejoicing. There was something disconcerting about the Emperor's enthusiasm. Macarius knew that things would not be left as they stood. The place could not be kept for his own meditations or the edification of his local congregation. There would be pilgrims. Something must be done to protect the holy places, something, also, to accommodate visitors. But "the finest church in the world, better than every other in every detail"—these words from the man who had already staggered the Empire with his scale of church building, who in Rome alone had spent the pay-roll of an army, who was now planning prodigious erections at Byzantium—these words from such a man were exorbitant. What did Macarius, a provincial clergyman who had spent most of his life dodging the police, know of porphyry and gold leaf?

Everyone was exceedingly civil to him. The Governor and the architect Dracilianus and all the contractors and clerks-of-the-works seemed to defer to

him, and yet helplessly he felt that everything was
being spoiled.

If only the Imperial architects had not been consumed with this passion for symmetry! No sooner
had Dracilianus surveyed the site, than he spoke of
levelling and orientating it. He failed to hide his
annoyance that the sepulchre did not lie dead west
of Calvary and even hinted that perhaps this might
be arranged; there at least Macarius was obdurate.
What Dracilianus finally did, however, was nearly
as bad. Macarius was shown the plans and the eleva-
tions, he was told a multitude of technical terms. He
consented now knowing what was proposed. And
at once the holy places swarmed with workmen.
There were barrows and gang-planks and scaffolding
everywhere; the whole area was screened from observation and though Macarius had the entrée he found
himself lost among dust and industry.

Months later Dracilianus's plan was revealed.
Everything was transformed. Where Hadrian had
levelled up, he had levelled down. Taking the floor
of the sepulchre as his mean Dracilianus had created
a new, perfectly flat platform. The hill in which the
sepulchre stood had been cut away, leaving only a
thin, geometrically regular mass of stone round the
sepulchre itself so that what had been a cave was
now a tiny house. The hill of Calvary had been

trimmed to a cube; it lay outside the future basilica, which was strictly orientated on the axis of the tomb. There were pegs and lines and trenches everywhere marking the proposed buildings. The basilica was to contain neither of the holy places, but to stand in a great, rectangular, colonnaded yard five hundred feet long. To the east of it a separate, semi-circular building was to enclose the tomb. It would require, in all, eighty columns, the architect explained, great quantities of marble and cedarwood. He rather fancied he had hit off just what the Emperor had in mind. He had quite outdone the Lateran basilica.

But Macarius lacked vision of these future architectural glories. He had seen clearly enough the mourning women on the lonely hill-side; he could not see the eighty columns. He saw only a parade ground cluttered with two incongruous protuberances, a sort of hut and an empty pedestal. He was lost, far from home, in this wilderness of mensuration. What Hadrian had carelessly preserved, Constantine had zealously destroyed, it seemed to Macarius.

And now came news that the Empress Dowager was on her way to visit them.

"You see what you've done," said the Prefect. "I hope you're satisfied."

CHAPTER ELEVEN

Epiphany

Hᴇʀᴇ, as elsewhere, little was known of the Empress
Dowager. She was a golden legend. They expected
someone very old and very luxurious; and they rather
hoped, gentle. Instead they met a crank; and more
than a crank, a saint. It was altogether too much.
They were prepared to meet demands for delicacies
of the table and elaborate furniture. They had se-
cured quite a passable orchestra from Alexandria.
What Helena wanted was something of quite another
order. She wanted the True Cross.

On the day of her arrival she made it clear that
they had miscalculated. They went out to meet her,
Bishop and Prefect and the whole city in a great
cavalcade. They surrounded her litter with a massed
choir and so led her to Government House. This
was a nondescript huddle of buildings comprising
the old Antonia Tower, part of Herod's palace and
more recent military offices. Nothing very much
could be done with the exterior but the upper rooms
had been lavishly upholstered. Helena, alighting,

seemed to regard the place critically. The major-domo—imported with the band from Egypt—tried to put a good face on it by remarking that this was originally Pilate's Praetorium. It might have been. No one was quite sure. On the whole most people thought that it was, though certainly much altered. Helena was plainly impressed. The major-domo went further. These marble steps, he explained, were the identical stairway which Our Lord had descended on his way to death. The effect was beyond his expectation. The aged Empress knelt down, there and then in her travelling cloak, and painfully and prayerfully climbed the twenty-eight steps on her knees. More than this, she made the whole of her suite follow her example. Next day she ordered her private cohort of sappers to take the whole staircase to pieces, number them, crate them and pack them on wagons. "I am sending it to Pope Sylvester," she said. "A thing like this ought to be in the Lateran. You clearly do not attach proper importance to it here."

Then, having rendered Government House uninhabitable she bade her court find billets where they could, and herself settled in a single small room among the nuns of Mount Zion where she did her own housework and took her turn in waiting at table.

The Holy Stairs left for the coast in a train of

wagons. Macarius and his chapter watched them go aghast. Royal collectors had been known to strip whole provinces of their works of art. The Church of Jerusalem had unique treasures—the crown of thorns, the lance, the shroud and many others. Were they to lose now, in the hour of liberation, what they had guarded so devotedly through all the years of persecution? They conferred and decided to make one great present. They would thus at the same time express their loyalty to the throne and emphasize their right of possession in all they had. They gave Helena the Holy Coat, which a soldier won at dice and sold later to a disciple. The Empress was grateful but it was not what she really wanted. She wanted one thing only. Meanwhile, she set a squad to work loading some tons of common earth. The fancy had taken her to build a church in Rome at the Sessorian Palace and to lay its foundations in the soil of the Holy Land. Macarius watched this operation without alarm.

It was soon evident that the Empress's change of address did not presage a regime of pious seclusion. The old lady was out and about everywhere, every day. She rode to Bethlehem. Here a small Christian community had charge of the cave of the Nativity. They used it for Mass and had built a little meeting house over its entrance. Hither at Christmas all the Christians of Jerusalem came with their Bishop to keep the vigil. "Just the place for a basilica," said Helena and, behold, in a few weeks the work began. She started, too, to build on Olivet. This, they told her, was a family estate of St. Joachim and St. Ann. Old trees grew here whose fruits they had enjoyed. Here was their family burial-place. Our Lady had played here as a child and here her body had briefly lain, shrouded and anointed. Here lay the gardens where Jesus had resorted and the cave where he had taken shelter often with the apostles; here he had passed the night in agony before his arrest, and hence he had ascended to heaven. It was as holy a place as any in Jerusalem. "Just the place for a basilica."

Helena visited the sites often, saw the first trenches cut and picnicked among her foundations. And Macarius saw his little diocese growing vast in wealth and importance and fading from his recognition, as Dracilianus reduced everything to symmetry and covered the rough, the real, stone with panels of marble.

It was like a masque of oriental magic, this utterance of a spell, this materialization from the clouds of domes and colonnades. Helena said the word, the complex machinery of imperial engineering was set into motion and she returned to help wash dishes in the convent scullery. It was, rather, a part of all that preternatural fecundity that surrounded her; of that Second Spring of unfailing clemency, when the seed germinated overnight, struck deep root and by noon threw up strong stems and a waving cumulus of flower and foliage. The multivarious harvest spiced the air and brought balm to her fretful hours. For she was fretful at times because she sought something quite different; not the budding sapling but old, seasoned wood.

She went about her quest with a single mind, questioning everyone. There were timber merchants in the town who had come there with tenders for new work, many of them local firms who had been in the business for generations. None of them, however, claimed any experience in the matter of making gallows. They were quite willing to try, they said. What sort of wood was used for crosses three hundred years ago? It was a question they had not considered. The district was well wooded then, as now, they said. You could take your pick. All agreed, with professional assurance, that there was nothing like sound timber for endurance. All could quote instances of woodwork which had outlived concrete and masonry. "Only gets the harder with age, ma'am," they declared. "No reason why it shouldn't last for ever provided it isn't burnt and the insects don't get at it. There aren't many insects in these parts but there's been a power of burning."

She sent for historians and antiquaries. Some had already arrived in the town, hearing of the Empress's foible. Others came at her invitation from Alexandria and Antioch, Christian, Jewish and heathen, all eager to help.

The Christians were full of information. "It is generally believed," a Coptic elder assured her, "that the cross was compounded of every species of wood so that all the vegetable world could participate in the act of redemption."

"Oh, nonsense," said Helena.

"Of course," said the Copt, highly delighted. "So I have always maintained. That is to put a complexion altogether too naturalistic and quantitative on the matter."

"Why must the vegetable world participate in this act, please?" asked a young clergyman from Italy. "It was in no way redeemed or susceptible of redemption."

"Surely, the mere carpentry of such a cross," said simple Macarius, whom Helena liked to have at hand on these occasions, "would have been so elaborate as to take many years? Some specimens of wood are known to come only from the forests far in the south of Africa and some from India."

"Exactly," said the Copt. "I have proved that the truth is much more simple. One arm was of box-wood, one of cypress, one of cedar and one of pine. These four woods symbolize . . ."

Another clergyman maintained the wood was aspen and that it was for this reason that the tree now continually shivered with shame. "Rot," said Helena.

A story still more elaborate was propounded by a swarthy scholar from the Upper Nile. When Adam was ill, he explained, his son Seth went to Paradise for some Oil of Mercy. The Archangel Michael gave him instead three seeds which arrived too late to save Adam from death. Seth put them in the corpse's mouth and from them grew three rods which Moses later came to possess. He employed them for a variety of magical purposes, including the blanching of Negroes, until in David's day they turned into a single tree. (Here Helena began to show signs of impatience.) Solomon cut the tree down and tried to use it in the roof of the temple but it would not fit any purpose. A lady named Maximilla sat on it accidentally and her clothes burst into flame, so Solomon whipped Maximilla to death and used the wood as a footbridge which the Queen of Sheba, crossing, at once detected.

"Oh, do stop," said Helena. "It's just this kind of story that I've come to disprove."

"There's a great deal more," said the darky, reproachfully. "At the end it floats up in the middle of the pool of Bethesda."

"Bosh," said Helena.

The Jews, Alexandrians of deep scholarship, showed more caution. Crucifixion, they remarked, was a Roman barbarity, quite alien to the best Jewish tradition. Their people, quite properly, stoned malefactors. The Gabaonites, indeed, had crucified the seven descendants of Saul, but that was in most exceptional circumstances—to make the barley grow —and very long ago. At the period which interested the Empress such a thing could not have occurred. She must really consult the Roman military historians.

One such was present. He said that pine was the cheapest wood and the easiest to work. No doubt that was what was used. Probably the upright was a more or less permanent fixture. The beam which the victim carried to his execution would be the cross-piece, which would be hoisted, with him hanging, to a socket and bolted into place. The same cross was no doubt used countless times.

Here the Jews interposed. That was not possible, they said. The execution was a Roman action but it had taken place on Jewish soil at the time when Jewish law was still paramount. And the law was perfectly clear on this subject. Anything connected with a violent death was unclean and liable to contaminate the neighbourhood. Instruments of execution, even if only the litter of a stoning or the bloodless cord of a strangulation, had to be cleared away, right out of sight, that very day.

Well, whose business would that be?

The temple guards, said the Roman. Romans did not concern themselves with ritual observances of that sort.

The friends and family of the victim, said the Jews. In this case, apparently, they had been given charge of the body—a most unusual provision. No doubt all arrangements had been left to them.

The soldiers, said the Christians. It had been no ordinary execution. The city was in turmoil. There had been alarming portents. Special precautions were taken to seal and guard the tomb. Special precautions would have been taken to dispose of all relics.

Anyway, said the Roman, it was just one of those baffling little lacunae that occur in history, sacred or secular, and are never filled. There was no means now of learning precisely what happened then.

But in spite of all expert discouragement, Helena held to her purpose.

Macarius spoke little at these conferences. When they were over Helena sought his opinion. He gave it diffidently.

It was certainly not the disciples who had hidden the cross, he said. Had they done so, the memory would have been preserved in the lore of his church. Nothing had ever been known about the cross. That he could vouch for. Jew or Roman, who had hidden it, died with the secret.

"Very well," said Helena. "Let us argue from there. A party is detailed, temple guards or legionaries—we don't know which—to get rid of two large baulks of timber, quickly and unobtrusively. What do they do? Clearly they don't attract attention or waste time by carrying them far. The ground all round is rocky. They could not dig a trench big enough to hide them. What do they look for? A

cave or the cellar of a ruined house—something like
that. The place is full of them. Wherever I've been,
I've seen them. All we have to do is to search all
the hiding-places of that kind round Calvary and
we are bound to find it."

"My dear lady," said Macarius, "your Majesty,
ma'am. Have you studied the ground round Calvary?"

"Not very much. It's always been so full of builders
and people."

"Exactly. Come and look now."

They went together to the east end of the site,
where the rising ground afforded a general view of
the workings. It was near sundown and the men
were packing up for the day. At their feet lay the
flat waste space with its two little lumps, fenced
and covered in sacking. All over the site the first
beginnings of walls and piers, and beyond it and
round it for many times its area stretched the out-
works. There was the rubble and rock which had
been cleared away; there was the building stone
and marble which had been assembled; there were
brick kilns and lime kilns and concrete mixers; there
were huge wooden cranes; wagons and hand-carts;
the stables of draught horses and the barracks of the
labourers; field kitchens and latrines; drawing-office

and book-keeper's office; the guarded strong room where the pay was kept; there were the shells of houses evacuated and half-demolished and the shells of temporary houses under construction. There was a network of causeways and cuttings; there was a whole street of booths where hucksters had set up shop to catch the men on pay-day before they reached the market. All this had been brought into being by the words: "Let's have a basilica."

In time, no doubt, order and reverence would return, so Macarius thought, but as he stood beside the Empress and showed her what was being done, he merely said: "Do you really think that in all this you will be able to find a hole in the ground and a piece of wood?"

"Oh yes, I think so," said Helena cheerfully.

Everyone in Jerusalem remarked on Helena's vigour. The old lady was positively indefatigable, they all said. But in truth she was very weary. Winter set in. The convent was exposed, damp and chill. It was not thus, in Dalmatia, that she had planned her old age. She seemed to have come to an end of her questions. No one was helpful. No one was hopeful. At Christmas she had not the strength to ride out with the procession to Bethlehem. She went to communion in the convent chapel and that day allowed the nuns to make a fuss of her, spending the feast crouched over a wood fire which they lit for her in her room.

But by Twelfth Night she rallied and on the eve set out by litter along the five rough miles to the shrine of the Nativity. There was no throng of pilgrims. Macarius and his people kept Epiphany in their own church. Only the little community of Bethlehem greeted her and led her to the room they had prepared. She rested there dozing until an hour before dawn when they called her and led her out under the stars, then down into the stable-cave, where they made a place for her on the women's side of the small, packed congregation.

The low vault was full of lamps and the air close and still. Silver bells announced the coming of the three vested, bearded monks, who like the kings of old now prostrated themselves before the altar. So the long liturgy began.

Helena knew little Greek and her thoughts were not in the words nor anywhere in the immediate scene. She forgot even her quest and was dead to everything except the swaddled child long ago and those three royal sages who had come from so far to adore him.

"This is my day," she thought, "and these are my kind."

Perhaps she apprehended that her fame, like theirs, would live in one historic act of devotion; that she too had emerged from a kind of ὀυτοπία or nameless realm and would vanish like them in the sinking nursery fire-light among the picture-books and the day's toys.

"Like me," she said to them, "you were late in coming. The shepherds were here long before; even the cattle. They had joined the chorus of angels before you were on your way. For you the primordial discipline of the heavens was relaxed and a new defiant light blazed amid the disconcerted stars.

"How laboriously you came, taking sights and calculating, where the shepherds had run barefoot! How odd you looked on the road, attended by what outlandish liveries, laden with such preposterous gifts!

"You came at length to the final stage of your pilgrimage and the great star stood still above you. What did you do? You stopped to call on King Herod. Deadly exchange of compliments in which there began that unended war of mobs and magistrates against the innocent!

"Yet you came, and were not turned away. You too found room before the manger. Your gifts were not needed, but they were accepted and put carefully by, for they were brought with love. In that new order of charity that had just come to life, there was room for you, too. You were not lower in the eyes of the holy family than the ox or the ass.

"You are my especial patrons," said Helena, "and patrons of all late-comers, of all who have a tedious journey to make to the truth, of all who are confused with knowledge and speculation, of all who through politeness make themselves partners in guilt, of all who stand in danger by reason of their talents.

"Dear cousins, pray for me," said Helena, "and for my poor overloaded son. May he, too, before the end find kneeling-space in the straw. Pray for the great, lest they perish utterly. And pray for Lactantius and Marcias and the young poets of Trèves and for the souls of my wild, blind ancestors; for their sly foe Odysseus and for the great Longinus.

"For His sake who did not reject your curious gifts, pray always for all the learned, the oblique, the delicate. Let them not be quite forgotten at the Throne of God when the simple come into their kingdom."

CHAPTER TWELVE
Ellen's Invention

PRESENTLY with the passing weeks the builders worked under a milder sky and cyclamen unfolded in the surrounding hills. But Helena took no comfort in the return of Spring; she had come to the end of all her questions.

Lent suited her mood better. It was a season not yet standardized in its austerity. At Jerusalem, where they kept holiday on Saturday as well as on Sunday, there were eight five-day weeks of fasting. And when Macarius said "fast" he meant quite simply "starve." Other dioceses indulged in mitigations—wine, oil, milk, little snacks of olives and cheese—which allowed the faithful to maintain a state of continuous rabbit-like nibbling. In Jerusalem if a man wished to attain the rewards of fasting he lived on water and thin gruel and nothing else. Some kept the full five days on this fare; many took Wednesdays off and dined heavily; others, weaker still, dined on Tuesdays and Thursdays. It was left to each to judge his own capacity. But if he did fast, he must fast thoroughly; that was Macarius's rule.

Helena was exempted by her age from all obligation. Nevertheless she decided to fast. It seemed to her a matter of practical expediency. Her interrogations had come to nothing. She had exhausted all the natural means of finding what she sought. "Very well," she said, "I'll see what fasting will do."

The nuns vainly begged her to consider her health. They did so with good reason for as the weeks slowly passed she grew weak and sometimes lightheaded. When Saturdays and Sundays came she had no inclination to eat much. By the beginning of Holy Week she was barely recognizable as the formidable woman who had cross-examined the archaeologists.

Palm Sunday was a day of heavy trial. Mass at dawn, a procession to Olivet, a whole day moving about the hillside from one holy place to another. Finally they re-enacted the entry into Jerusalem, Macarius walking on a leaf-strewn path, back to the sepulchre for vespers. At the end of that day Helena was too weary to eat the supper the convent had prepared, but crept instead shivering to bed.

All building stopped for Holy Week. The whole Christian population gave themselves up to devotions which became daily more strenuous. On Thursday evening there was another procession to and around Olivet. Helena followed the routine resolutely on foot, the candle firm in her hand but with a mind which often grew dizzy and blank among the lections and psalmody. They ended the night in Gethsemane, where the gospel was sung recounting the agony and the arrest of Christ. At the final words the whole multitude burst out into lamentation, part customary, part spontaneous, a great swell of wailing and groaning. The candles were all out now and day just breaking. The sad procession shuffled back through the gates of the city to begin the long obsequies on the site of Calvary.

At the end of the Good Friday office Helena withdrew in solitude to her room. The tragedy was over. The stone had been rolled across the mouth of the tomb. The disciples had slunk away each with his woe and shame. Pilate slept sound. After all the alarms of the day the city lay silent as the dead God in his shroud. All Helena's full heart was with the bereaved women of long ago.

The nuns brought her some gruel which she left untasted. They whispered about her, the feverish fixed look of her eye, the trembling of all her limbs. One of them brought her a syrup of opium and this she accepted. She had slept little in the past week.

Now she lay quite relaxed at last, like the body in the tomb.

All her life Helena's sleep had been full of dreams and always, daily, even on the far-off hunting mornings of her youth, she opened her eyes on a scene of loss; her waking heart momentarily drawn tight with the pain of leave-taking; then swiftly eased. Now on the most desolate night of the year there came to her, as though she were waking to clear day rather than, as was the case, sinking into deeper sleep, a dream that she knew was of God.

She dreamed she was up and about, alone in the lane which skirted the wall of Solomon's Temple. The place was no longer thronged as it always was by day nor cloudy with dust, but quite empty and silent and brilliant as a mountain peak. Helena knew she was young again and gaily greeted a man who approached up the lane as though he had been one of her father's subjects and she riding out to hunt. When he answered "Good morning, miss," the words seemed natural and proper on that timeless morning.

He seemed middle-aged and was dressed and bearded like an orthodox Jew.

"You have come to lament at the Temple wall?"

"Not me, lady. You mustn't judge me by these

togs. I only put them on once in a while when I
come here to see how the old place is getting along.
I've been abroad a long time, travelling all over
the place. It's broadened my mind. They're a narrow
lot the Jews you meet round here. I ought to know.
I was one of them once. Had a little shop just down
that street. Not much of a place, but I might never
have moved if it hadn't been for the Romans busting
the place up. Believe me, lady, I'm grateful to them."

Helena knew that this day of their meeting was
marked on no calendar. "You must be very old,"
she said.

"I'll say I am. You'd never guess how old."

She looked hard at him and saw that on this morning of renewal he had no youth. His skin was smooth
as basalt, his hair barely tinged with grey; his body
was stocky and robust, but for all his cheerful impu-
dence of speech his eyes were weary and cold as a
crocodile's. "First it was old Titus who bust it up.
All my business ruined. I built it up again bit by bit.
Then more troubles. Everything bust up again. Well,
I'd had enough that time. Twice was too often for
yours truly. So I took to my travels and since then
I've had my ups and downs but I've never looked
back. I dress like this when I'm here because that's
my way. I always make a point of doing what's done

wherever I am. I've worn yellow trousers in Bordeaux and wolf-skins in Germany. You should see me in Persia at the court. Adaptability—that's the secret of a personal business like mine.

"I'm in incense, see. There's no finer connexion. All the leading shrines are on my books. They know I handle the right stuff. Buy it myself in Arabia, ship it myself. Besides, they all like dealing with me because I'm reverent, see. Whatever it is they worship —monkeys, snakes: I've seen some pretty queer goings-on in Phrygia, I can tell you—I always respect religion. It's my bread and butter.

"It's a very particular trade, mine. You have to keep your ears open, especially these days when there's always some new cult starting; some new temple going up. That's why I'm here today. They were talking about Jerusalem in the bazaars in the Hadramaut, how the Romans were putting up a new temple here—to the Galilean of all people. That took me back a bit. Took me back three hundred years to be exact. Why, it's all on account of the Galilean that I'm here today."

"You knew him?"

"Well, in a manner of speaking, no. I was thick with the Sanhedrin at the time. It wouldn't have been good for business to get mixed up with the Galilean in those days. How things change.

"He came right past the shop the day he was executed. Stumbled just on my doorstep. He was all in. They had to get a man to help with the cross after that. Mind you I didn't hold with crucifying him. Live and let live, I say. Still I couldn't have him there on my doorstep, could I, so I moved him on quick. 'Come on,' I said, 'none of that now. This is no place for the likes of you.' He just looked at me, not exactly a nasty look, but as if he wanted to be sure of knowing me again. Then he said: 'Tarry till I come.' It didn't sound much at the time but I've thought about it a lot since and believe me, lady, I've had plenty of time to think. I wasn't fifty at the time and from that day to this I've never felt a day older. Queer, isn't it? You'd think I'd know everything about religion, seeing the business I'm in, but I don't. There are still things I find queer.

"I stopped counting birthdays after the hundred and fiftieth. Up till then it was rather exciting seeing everyone else dying off. Then somehow I lost interest. No one would believe me and anyway they wouldn't be happy doing business with a man of my age. They'd think I knew too much. One loses count of everything after a time. Women first; even money in the end."

"Tell me more about that day."

"I didn't like it," said the businessman. "To be quite frank I didn't like it at all. It got dark. There was an earthquake—nothing much, but coming on top of everything else it made people jittery. They said they saw ghosts. It was a very queer sort of day. No business. After a time I locked up the shop and went to see what was going on, but by the time I arrived it was all over. They were taking the bodies down."

As they talked the Empress and the business man walked up the lane to the place where the basilica was being built. "Think of it. All this money being spent on him after all this time. That's what makes my business so interesting—always a surprise."

"What happened to the cross?" asked Helena.

"Oh, they threw those away, all three of them. They had to, you know, by law."

"Where did they put them? Do you remember?"

"Yes."

"I want that cross."

"Yes, come to think of it I expect there'll be quite a demand for anything to do with the Galilean now that he's suddenly become so popular and respectable."

"Could you show me where it is?"

"I reckon so."

"I am rich. Tell me your price."

"I wouldn't take anything from you, lady, for a little service like that. I shall get paid all right, in time. You have to take a long view in my business. How I see it, this new religion of the Galilean may be in for quite a run. A religion starts, no one knows how. Soon you get holy men and holy places springing up everywhere, old shrines change their names, there's apparitions and pilgrimages. There'll be ladies wanting other things besides the cross. All one wants is to get the thing started properly. One wants a few genuine relics in thoroughly respectable hands. Then everyone else will follow. There won't be enough genuine stuff to meet the demand. That will be my turn. I shall get paid. I wouldn't take anything from you now, lady. Glad to see you have the cross. It won't cost you a thing."

Helena listened and in her mind saw, clear as all else on that brilliant timeless morning, what was in store. She saw the sanctuaries of Christendom become a fair ground, stalls hung with beads and medals, substances yet unknown pressed into sacred emblems; heard a chatter of haggling in tongues yet unspoken. She saw the treasuries of the Church filled with forgeries and impostures. She saw Christians fighting and stealing to get possession of trash. She saw all this, considered it and said: "It's a stiff price"; and then: "Show me the cross."

"They threw it in an old underground cistern," said the business man. "One just outside the gate. A big place down some steps. It used to be the main water supply for this end of the city but it dried up for some reason years before."

"Where?"

Without hesitation the Jew led her to the western edge of the new platform and beyond it among the heaped-up rubble.

"It's hard to tell exactly," he said. "They've altered the place so much."

He took a sight through his weary, knowing eyes at the two fixed points in that scene of change—the tomb and the summit of Golgotha. He judged the distance carefully and at length dug in a heel. "Dig here," he said. "You won't be far out. Dig till you come on the steps."

Then Helena awoke and found that she was an old woman, alone and slightly drugged, in the dark. She lay waiting for the dawn with prayers of hope and thankfulness.

When it was light she went to the sepulchre. People were already assembling for the first office of Holy Saturday. She was a familiar figure there and excited no comment.

She followed the path she had taken in her dream, climbed the heap and stood where she had stood with the businessman. Where she had seen him set his heel there was a print in the dust that looked as though it had been left by a goat's hoof. Helena gently rubbed it out and set in its place her own mark, a little cross of pebbles.

The new excavation was begun immediately after Easter. Helena came down to watch the work and herself ceremoniously filled the first basket of rubble. Her command was absolute but no one on the site welcomed this interruption of the routine. To the clerk-of-the-works there seemed no limit to the delays this whimsical old lady might impose and even the labourers were resentful. It might be thought that it was nothing to them, sweating and straining to order, eyes on the ground, what they were doing or why. But the work had reached a stage when it was intelligible; the plan of the massive walls was clear, and the men had begun to feel pride in their share of this historic undertaking. Now they were called off to shift the rubble they had themselves laboriously deposited; to look for a dry reservoir.

There was grumbling in the barrack-rooms and in the drawing-office. Bishop Macarius, too, was sad to see the confusion further prolonged; the return to regular worship further postponed. Nevertheless the work was done, not cheerfully but with Roman method and discipline.

They were digging the lower, westward slope of the hill of Golgotha. Under their own new rubbish they found great masses of old masonry from the city wall that had been thrown down there. Under the masonry lay the original rock and there, just where Helena had pointed, they came on the steps and the low arch where in the time of the Maccabees women had come to fill their pitchers and caravans had paused to water before entering the city. The entrance was blocked to the roof and here, on Helena's orders, pick and spade were put away and wooden shovels issued which would do less injury to the wood, if they struck it. The rubbish was scrutinized as it went into the baskets and any fragment of timber carefully set aside. In this way they worked their way slowly deeper until, towards the end of April, to the surprise of all except Helena they came to the reservoir. Torch-light showed them a large ruinous cellar, littered waist deep with the detritus of fallen vaulting. This seemed the chamber they sought and the whole gang became at once eager and interested. Helena had an ivory chair carried down and there she sat, attended by one nun, hour by hour in the flare and smoke and dust, watching the men at work.

It took many days. The roof threatened to subside and they worked like miners propping it as they advanced. Basketful by basketful the rubbish was carried away, sifted and tipped. Helena sat on her little throne watching and praying. Two days before the end it became evident that there was nowhere now where the large timbers she sought could be concealed. But she showed no dismay. When at length the whole chamber was clear and swept and quite empty. Helena sat on, praying.

The nun said: "Don't you think, ma'am, that perhaps we ought to go home?"

"Why? We have not found what we came for."

"But, ma'am, it isn't here. You can't always trust dreams, you know. Some are sent by the devil."

"My dream was all right."

The clerk-of-the-works came to ask permission to dismiss the workmen. "It is already quite dark outside," he said.

"That makes no difference down here."

"But, ma'am, what is there for them to do?"

"Search."

The old lady rose from her chair and attended by the linkman made a slow inspection of the vault. At the south-west corner she tapped with her cane on the wall.

"Look at this," she said. "There's been a door here and someone botched it up in a hurry."

The clerk-of-the-works examined the corner. "Yes," he said, "there certainly seems to have been something here."

"I think I can guess whose work this was. After the stone had been rolled back from the tomb the High Priests made sure nothing else was going to escape. In my country we call that locking the stable door after the horse has been stolen."

"Yes, ma'am. That is a most interesting speculation. Perhaps tomorrow."

"I don't leave this cellar until I've seen what's the other side of that wall," said Helena. "Call for volunteers. We only want a small gang on this job. And see that they're all Christians. We don't want any heathen around at a time like this."

So Helena stayed in prayer while the wall was broken down. It was a simple task and when it fell the stone went rolling away down into the darkness out of sight. This passage was steep and quite clear of rubbish. The men stood back in hesitation.

"Go on," said Helena. "You'll find a cross in there. Perhaps more than one. Bring them up carefully. I will stay here. I've a few more prayers to say."

The little torch-lit party disappeared. Helena heard their cautious stumbling steps descend, grow faint and presently return.

The leading torch-bearer appeared at the entrance, after him two men carrying a baulk of timber.

"There are several more bits, ma'am."

"Bring them all up. Lay them here. The Bishop shall see them in the morning. Give these men a lot of money," she said rather dizzily to the clerk-of-the-works. "Set a guard on the wood." And taking the nun by the hand seeking support and guidance she said: "So it is finished."

Next day, the 3rd of May, Bishop Macarius and Helena examined her finds. They were laid out on the pavement of the new basilica and comprised in order of importance the members of three crosses, detached but well-preserved, a notice board split into two, four nails and a triangular block of wood. Half the notice board which bore, ill-scrawled in the three great tongues of the ancient world, the supreme

Title, was still attached to one of the taller posts.

"So we can be quite certain about *that* one," said Helena briskly.

Now that her quest was at last accomplished all sentiment was dead and she was as practical about arrangements as though some new furniture had been delivered at her house.

"The nails go with the Holy Cross," she decided, "and that I take to be a footrest."

"Very likely, ma'am."

"Now for the cross-beams. We must see which belongs to which. Get one of the carpenters. He ought to be able to help."

But the carpenter said there was no way of knowing. It was a rough job anyway. Nothing fitted. "God alone knows," he said, "which piece is supposed to fit where."

"Then God will show us," said Helena.

"Your highness, ma'am, dear lady," said Macarius. "You really must not expect miracles every day."

"Why not?" said Helena. "There wouldn't be any point in God giving us the cross if He didn't want us to recognize it. Find someone ill, very ill," she said, "and try the cross-beams on him."

It worked, as everything had worked for Helena

on this remarkable tour. The beams were carried up to the room of a dying woman and laid one at a time beside her on the bed. Two made no difference. The third effected a complete recovery.

"So now we know," said Helena.

Then she set about the division of the property. Half was for Macarius; half for the rest of the world. She took the cross-beam of the True Cross and left him the upright. She gave him the part of the Title which was inscribed in Hebrew. All four nails she set aside for Constantine. The triangular block of wood was of more doubtful value. It might be the suppedaneum if a suppedaneum had been used. On the other hand it might just be a block of wood. But she added it to her baggage and gave boundless pleasure later by presenting it to the uncritical Cypriots. The other crosses proved to be indistinguishable. One belonged to the repentant thief, one to his blaspheming fellow; but which was which? Patients less gravely afflicted, people even with minor nervous troubles, were successively paraded, touched with the wood and sent away quite unrelieved. Only a Briton could have solved the problem as Helena did. Calling to the carpenter she ordered him to split all four pieces and to construct a composite pair of crosses each of which should comprise a half of each original. When this was done she gave one to Macarius and retained the other.

Meanwhile the beacons blazed news of the discovery to the capital and post-horsemen carried it through Christendom. Te Deums were sung in the imperial basilicas. No one who watched that day, while the Empress calmly divided her treasure, could have discerned her joy. Her work was finished. She had done what only the saints succeed in doing; what indeed constitutes their patent of sanctity. She had completely conformed to the will of God. Others a few years back had done their duty gloriously in the arena. Hers was a gentler task, merely to gather wood. That was the particular, humble purpose for which she had been created. And now it was done. So with her precious cargo she sailed joyfully away.

She sailed away, out of authentic history. Fishermen in the Adriatic say that she came there and when her galley was threatened with wreck, calmed the raging sea by throwing into it one of the sacred nails, since when those waters have always been kind to sailors.

The fishermen of Cyprus say that she performed this act off their own dangerous shore in the gulf of Satalia. She then landed, all Cypriots agree, and found this island dying of a drought that had lasted seventeen years. Since Catherine was martyred it had not rained in Cyprus. The ground was all baked and bare; the enterprising had left and found new homes abroad. All who were left of that once teeming population had grown brutal with hardship and murdered travellers who were cast up there on the supposition that they were Jews. Demons haunted the island and possessed it during the hours of darkness so that it was impossible to bury the dead who, as soon as they were decently covered, were disinterred and thrown back putrefying on their old doorsteps.

For these people Helena set up one of the composite crosses of the thieves and at once the drought broke so that she was obliged to build a bridge, which may still be seen, in order to pass what, when she arrived, had been a dry gulley. She sawed up the suppedaneum, if suppedaneum it was, and made two little crosses of it, which she gave the islanders and at once the demons left, gyring up in a noisy flock until they dwindled to the size of starlings and were lost in the upper air. Then she summoned a new population from the neighbouring islands, mainly from Telos, and settled them on the now fertile land.

The cross which she left was put up in a church where it hovered, without support, for centuries, till the infidels took the island. She continued her voyage calling none knows where, for the people of those abandoned shores have taken her into their hearts and made her one with all great and beneficent ladies of myth and memory. In their poetry her cargo multiplied and was enriched with all the spoils of fairyland.

At length she came to Constantine whom she found in his new city. Vast gimcrack ministries were rising about him with reckless speed. At the moment he was chiefly occupied with a monument to himself, a porphyry column of unprecedented height on a huge white pedestal. On the summit of this he purposed to erect the colossal bronze Apollo of Pheidias which he had lately imported from Athens. The holy nails arrived opportunely for Constantine had decapitated the great statue, poised a portrait of himself on the neck and was even at that moment supervising the construction of the halo which was to surmount the whole. One of the nails was set as a ray shining from the imperial cranium.

Constantine had lately become interested in relics. He had brought the Palladium itself from Rome and embedded it in the foundations of his monument.

"I'm glad you are starting with a part of Troy," said Helena. "Your grandfather Coel will be pleased."

"I've got plenty of other things just as important," said Constantine. "Such a bit of luck. Just when I was laying the foundation-stone a dealer turned up from Palestine with a first-class collection. Really important stuff. I bought the lot, of course. It included Noe's adze—the very one he used on the ark—and Mary Magdalen's alabaster box and all sorts of things."

"And what have you done with them, my son?"

"They're all there, in the base of the column Nothing will ever shake it now."

He was delighted with his nails. The second he stuck in his hat. The third he put to a still more idiosyncratic use. He sent it to the smith and had it forged into a snaffle for his horse. When Helena heard this she was at first a little taken aback. But presently she smiled, giggled and was heard to utter the single, enigmatic word "stabularia."

Her strength was failing fast, and soon it became necessary for her to make her will. She disposed of everything in great detail, sending the Holy Coat to her old home at Trèves, a great piece of the Cross and the Title to her new church in the Sessorian Palace, dividing and dispersing her treasury so that no friends were forgotten. The bodies of the Magi, which had somewhere somehow got into her luggage, she is thought to have sent to Cologne. At last she emptied the whole cornucopia and there was nothing for her to leave except her own weary body. This Constantine wanted for his Church of the Apostles where the cenotaphs stood in a great circle, all empty and without worship. But Helena had decided where she would lie and her last act was to bequeath herself to Rome. She died on the 18th of August, 328. They carried her body to Rome and laid it in the sarcophagus Constantine had designed for himself, in the mausoleum he had built three miles out of The City on the road to Palestrina. There she lay undisturbed until the reign of Pope Urban VIII, when her bones were moved to the church of Ara Coeli where they lie today. Within a few yards of her, on the steps of that church, Edward Gibbon later sat and premeditated his history.

Helena's many prayers seem to have received unequal answers. Constantine was at long last baptized and died in the expectation of an immediate, triumphal entry to Paradise. Britain for a time became Christian, and 136 parish churches, a great part of them in the old lands of the Trinovantes, were dedicated to Helena. The Holy Places have been alternately honoured and desecrated, lost and won, bought and bargained for, throughout the centuries. But the wood had endured. In splinters and shavings gorgeously encased it has travelled the world over and found a joyous welcome among every race. For it states a fact.

Hounds are checked, hunting wild. A horn calls clear through the covert. Helena casts them back on the scent.

Above all the babble of her age and ours, she makes one blunt assertion. And there alone is Hope.